Praise for *No One*

"The words are simple yet they have tremendous power. You want to turn down the corner of every page so you can go back to particular moments, reread phrases that have made you shiver."

—*Le Figaro Litteraire*

"A cubist, polyphonic portrait of great elegance and restraint, [*No One*] is two autobiographies in one, father and daughter. Its language is a delicate fabric of impressions and memories, re-creating images of a complex, attractive man who remained a stranger both to the world and to himself."

—*Le Monde des Livres*

"[Aubry's] words, like a string of melancholy diamonds, convey both her persistence and her inability to save her father . . . She need not worry: with this powerful book she has paid her debt of love in full."

—*Le Point*

"Page after page, meticulously and with infinite tenderness, [Aubry] explores this man's biography, his thoughts, his terrible breakdowns, his sense of dread."

—*Télérama*

NO ONE

a novel

NO ONE

a novel

GWENAËLLE AUBRY

translated by Trista Selous

Tin House Books

Portland, Oregon & New York, New York

This work, published as part of a program providing publication assistance, received financial support from the French Ministry of Foreign Affairs, the Cultural Services of the French Embassy in the United States, and FACE (French American Cultural Exchange). www.frenchbooknews.com

French Voices Logo designed by Serge Bloch

Published by Tin House Books, Portland, Oregon, and New York, New York

Distributed to the trade by Publishers Group West, 1700 Fourth St., Berkeley, CA 94710, www.pgw.com

Library of Congress Cataloging-in-Publication Data

Aubry, Gwenaëlle, 1971-

[Personne. English]

Personne : a novel / Gwenaelle Aubry ; translated by Trista Selous. – 1st U.S. ed.

    p. cm.

ISBN 978-1-935639-22-0

I. Selous, Trista, 1957- II. Title.

PQ2661.U225P4713 2012

843'.92–dc23

                                2011046506

First U.S. edition 2012

Printed in the USA

Interior design by Janet Parker and Jakob Vala

www.tinhouse.com

Introduction

In case you dwell on the American side of the Atlantic, let me catch you up on a recent development in international literature—*l'autofiction.*

L'autofiction is the French term for the stylized hybridization of fiction and autobiography as applied in contemporary literature. It's in relatively wide circulation, this coinage, dreamed up, originally, by one Serge Doubrovsky in 1977, perhaps as a term of self-discovery, or of literary politics. The movement waited for about a generation to lift off, however. By now, l'autofiction is nearly pandemic, at least continentally speaking. An uncharitable critique of contemporary literature, perhaps along the lines of David Shields's recent manifesto on the value of nonfiction, *Reality Hunger*, would find in these particular tea leaves a draining away of the power of imagination.

8

But this *reality hunger* reading would dramatically miss the nuance in contemporary French literature–the way the writers of France occasionally situate themselves, paradoxically, oxymoronically, between autobiography and fiction, between genres, finding in this impulse the liberty that is released by recombination. L'autofiction is all about this nuance, this historical wisdom; it's about exploiting the energy of uncertainty and possibility between the imaginary and the documentary, in the process staying close to the human intention that is *language*, which is not, after all, a creature of genres.

Gwenäelle Aubry's *No One* coincides with this revolution in French contemporary writing. The title in French, *Personne*, makes clear its multiple layers. *Personne* literally means *no one*, but it also has traces of the Latinate *persona*, and the Etruscan *phersu*, mask, and the English *person*.

The story is simple. The father of the narrator of *No One*, the father of one Gwenäelle Aubry, is an intellectual of some heft and import who, in the middle of his life's journey, becomes episodically, seriously, progressively, mentally ill. Not just a little bit mentally ill, but deeply, psychotically, unstably mentally ill, given to flights of free association and impulsive behavior of a kind that jeopardizes the maturation of his two daughters. The causative event of *No One*, the engine of its alphabetical recollections of his multiple personae, is Aubry's discovery, after the death of her father, of a self-composed manuscript that attempts to detail his life and times. Through this manuscript, (and in it and with it), she attempts to make peace with her father.

It's possible that this is a precisely realistic account of Ms. Aubry's life, and of her father, Francois-Xavier Aubry–this story as described. But if it were an entirely realistic account in, for example, the literature of the country where I am writing these lines, it would likely be organized in relentless dramatic scenes involving Aubry, her sister, and her mother (all but absent here), or perhaps a bevy of friends who exist so that Aubry can talk to *someone* about all the horrible, strange, but ultimately *loveable* things that her father has done. We would get fully dramatized accounts, progressive stages of paternal unreliability, sentimental flights of description. This would be the *reality programming* edition of *No One*, perfectly calibrated for the tastes of voyeurs.

But this is not the account we have at all. The alpha and omega of *No One* is a life in linguistic traces. *No One* is not only aware of l'autofiction and of the way that French literature has played out recently, but it is also fully cognizant of the philosophical and theoretical pretexts that undergird some of what l'autofiction wants to do. We might speak, for example, of the way the later work of Roland Barthes, particularly, *A Lover's Discourse* (or *Fragments d'un discours amoureux*, as it is known on that side of the ocean), with its alphabetical organization of fragmentary meditations on love, prepares the way for Aubry's work. *No One* would not exist in the form it is in were it not for Barthes, but, still, that is only to describe its most manifest layer and to miss so much of what is really going on in the grave, stately sadness of its pages.

No One therefore begins with textual ramifications (with *écriture*), with a fragmentary but heavily quoted manuscript by Francois-Xavier Aubry, above which and beyond which exists the second text, the narrator's own, by a lucid and wise French writer who also studied philosophy, and who knows her Barthes, and her Deleuze, and her French psychonalysis. But there's a third layer, too. The opening of *No One* features a recitation (a *récit*) of the facts surrounding Antonin Artaud's incarceration, in the midforties, at a rather severe and draconian mental hospital situated in Rodez. Artaud is a shadow character in Aubry's novel, or a shadow text, so that this autofiction, if that's what it is, is full of shadows, full of analogies, full of characters, full of texts, the apparatus of literature, even if its immediate concerns are the consciousnesses of two people, narrator and father. As such, it is short, it is compact, highly poeticized, highly philosophical, but with fields of implication that range distantly. Just as Artaud, these days, is considered a French poet, though most of what comprises his later output is in a poetical form because that is all that a paranoid schizophrenic can manage late in life, so too is *No One* poetical, and compact, because that is what a grief-stricken philosopher and intellectual, Gwenäelle Aubry, can manage when confronted with this father, real or imaginary, or neither, or both.

What makes this a great book, then, is first its recoiling from conventional storytelling. This is, rather, storytelling by implication, with a reliance on patient attention, and on the possibilities of language. And there *is* a certain kind of language required for such a task—the description of grief—a language haunted with loss, but one that is unsentimental and celebratory (in an unsimplistic way), one admirably obsessed with accuracy. As in this representative passage:

> He had such a love of order and ritual, finery and ceremony, he had played so often with his own death, that I was convinced, when it came, that he must have tried to give it

a form, to shape it in his own image and that of the life it had penetrated so deeply. In the little white room I opened boxes and files, flicked through his countless notebooks for the first time, found the blue folder and the manuscript it contained. And, on page 169, I read the words that gave his death a face: *I'm hoping for a pretty death.*

No One finds its pathos in this way, in the circling around, in a great many iterations of being and nonbeing, in returning and departing, darting and feinting into the father's manuscript and the particulars thereof, and beyond that manuscript, as well. Perhaps we have to speak of a Venn diagram in which the narrator's account and the father's account collide in just the right way, where there is nothing to do but gaze mournfully at the collisions, *les mots justes*, of their points of view, wherein is heartache, the very considerable heartache, that must swamp the daughter of the terribly distant father. A specter of a father. *No One* does not describe sentimental incident; it describes moments of insight into and out of which the cloudy agent of forgetting creeps, so that the effort to understand must be constantly repeated, even as there is a desire to notate and preserve. There's nothing tidy about this grief. There's no American-style closure. Which makes *No One* all the more genuine, all the more lasting.

Aubry won the Prix Femina for the book you are holding, which is a belated, midcareer example of literary justice. The book could have come only at this instance in her career, when she'd learned what she had learned from her earlier work, able, in midcareer, to know what a midcareer novelist knows, which is wisdom and patience and relinquishment.

A lot had to happen before this book could happen, and all kinds of struggle had to precede this hard, bright gem. But *No One* also won the Prix Femina because France understands and supports the language of a broader conception of psychology, and especially psychology in extremis (see, e.g., Artaud's late radio play, *To Have Done with the Judgment of God*, funded by the state radio), as it also understands that the form *No One* takes, this very French hybrid, is one direction where literature can go profitably. There is scarcely a better example of creative thinking about the form of literature now than what Aubry has composed here. It rises up out of the field of European contemporary writing with an uncanny clarity, and so we are extremely lucky now to have it, too, in English, in this fine translation by Trista Selous.

—RICK MOODY, September 2011

NO ONE

A

Antonin Artaud

On December 9, 1945, Antonin Artaud wrote, from Rodez, to Henri Parisot.

He complains of the army of spellbinders waiting to burst into him from all sides, to camp in his mind, feed on his flesh, and live off his life,

he says what it is to carry such an army inside him, to be a teeming, deserted land, to have nothing inside but a hell of outsiders,

he describes, worse than pain, than eternal hell, the exploding of his real *self.*

In this letter of December 9, 1945, he raves—we can call it that too—that he's Jesus nailed to the cross in Golgotha and then thrown on a dung heap; he's the blasphemer and the bishop of Rodez, St. Anthony, and Lucifer, and in the notebooks he fills that winter he also proclaims himself father-mother, man-woman, frenetic substance of all begettings, womb for countless daughters,

his body has taken on the dimensions of the entire universe, has become the adopted land of theogonies, his mind eludes him, but gathers into itself the whole history of humanity,

he is master of reality, possibility is what he decides, the infinite obeys him because, he says

reality, don't get it

he himself is reality, sonorous, overflowing, throbbing,

that he is also Antonin Artaud

M. Antonin Artaud, born September 4, 1896, in Marseille, to be precise,

he still notes, but it's of little interest, an idea at the back of his mind, an outdated thesis,

on the other hand one thing he does know, floating in all this wreckage, one calm, clear truth

to which you feel, when he utters it, that he could, for a moment, cling:

I'm a great poet, that's all.

In the winter of '45 Artaud had already been locked up for eight years. He had been in the asylum of Sotteville-lès-Rouen, in Sainte-Anne, where Lacan judged him "set" in his madness, forever incapable of writing, Ville-Evrard, where he was transferred from the ward for agitated inmates to that of the epileptics, then the senile, and then from the ward of the senile to that of the undesirable. In Rodez, where he arrived in February '43, half-starved and dressed like a tramp, he spoke of God with Dr. Latrémolière and poetry with Dr. Ferdière;

he translated Lewis Carroll, genuflected in the cathedral, and spat and crossed himself on passing pregnant women. He was also subjected to twelve hundred electric shocks in three years. He would emerge from these sessions broken, boneless, and formless, no nerves in his body, no blood in his head, in a *puddle state*. For weeks he would be *in pursuit of his being like a dead man alongside a living man who is no longer him*. But he started writing again, drawing, filling notebooks.

On December 10, 1945, the day after Artaud's letter to Henri Parisot, my father was born. I don't know when he was first hospitalized. I might have been able to find some record, perhaps, in one of his notebooks—black leather diaries, school exercise books, "rough books," blocks of headed notepaper from hotels, loose sheets, jottings on the back of lecture notes, enough to fill several cardboard boxes. Some could be ascribed the names of hospitals and nursing homes he'd spent time in—the la Roseraie notebooks, la Verrière notebooks, Epinay notebooks, and so on.

My father was not *a great poet, that's all*. He didn't enshrine his suffering in beauty and power, his madness in genius, didn't invent a language of consecration and conflagration. I've read some of his notebooks and forgotten them. All I know is that every day of his life—or almost—he wrote. Every morning, every evening, he'd sit down at his desk, light a Pall Mall or a Craven A—their ash burned holes in the pages—and try to reconstitute his life. No stories, apart from dreams, but accounts, overviews, to-do lists (*Phone the girls, pay the rent, hold on until tomorrow*, and the next day he would cross them out and write *DONE* in the margin), and, most of all,

diagrams, drawn and drawn again, straight lines split into
segments—of happiness, sadness, times with or without alcohol, with or without hospitalization—bristling with dates and
names, then, gradually, the straight lines become fewer and
fewer and there are series of upturned triangles, peaks and
troughs, crests and rifts, tracing the map of his melancholia
on the squared paper. All I retain of my father's life is its inner
relief, its seismographic translation. I would be no more able
(or willing) than he to recount it, to go through the names and
dates that make up this story in whose shadow I grew up. I
can follow its rugged geography, its imprecise geometry, with
my finger. I know these are the contours of the dark side, the
negative of my life, that its rifts correspond to his absences and
that, even at a distance, I fell into them with him. I don't know
who he was any more than he did. All I know is that every
morning, every evening, when he opened his notebooks, it
.was this he was looking for. These countless lines and—even
in his worst moments—elegant, regular characters weave the
net in which he tried to catch himself, or stretch the canvas on
which he was the empty center. This was what he wanted: to
grasp, catch, collar himself.

Somewhere—I don't know where—there's the story of
the golem who, because he could never find his clothes in
the morning, decided one evening to make a note of where
they were. When he woke up he was at last able to locate each
garment—trousers, jacket, hat—until the moment he realized
something was still missing: Myself, he wondered suddenly,
where did I leave myself? Where am I? This, I think, is what
my father used to do every morning. He would pick up his
cigarettes, pen, and notebook and he would wonder where

he'd left himself. He would reach out his hand and find tatters, patched suits, Harlequin coats. The masks of his inner theater would appear on the white paper—a motley, unsteady crowd: the Prodigal Son and the Spurned Lover, the Clown and the Pirate, the Cop and the Robber, the Monk and the Rake, the Bourgeois and the Tramp, the Sage and the Madman. But in all this he himself was absent. Sometimes he would attempt a portrait: he would list his qualities—name surname date of birth profession identifying marks—then suddenly stop, as though he didn't believe a word of it. Himself—where had he left himself? Where was he?

As you know, I was born to a human mother and father. My sisters have not got four legs, or animal faces or red eyes. Nor have my children. And I look like a human being too—on the somber side perhaps. I like grass, but I do not graze, and I live in a studio apartment looking out over the trees in Montmartre, just below the Sacré-Cœur. It is here that I am becoming aware of my life again. It must have contained things that have completely escaped me—because I did not seek them out.

The words I transcribe here are the beginning of a piece of writing called *The Melancholic Black Sheep*. Almost two hundred pages of careful handwriting, corrected and annotated all the way through. On the cover of the blue file that holds them my father had written, *To be novelized*. This work was intended for others, starting with my sister and me. He spent the last months of his life writing, in the little apartment we'd fixed up for him: a light, white room on the ground floor of a modern block, reached via an L-shaped hall with the kitchen,

bathroom, and closet opening off it, its end wall entirely filled
by a bay window looking out over a tree-lined path. The place
had something impersonal and reassuring about it, the way
some hotel rooms do. As soon as we saw it we knew he would
be all right there. We brought in furniture and ornaments res-
cued from the Drouot auction house, a large bookcase to hold
his law books and boxes full of his notebooks, a divan bed
and a desk, worn carpets, an Empire table, paintings by my
grandfather, a black-and-white photograph of the big house
at Saint-Méloir-des-Ondes—all relics of a dynasty of notables,
surrounding him with the décor of a slow-moving, cosseted,
respectable life. The psychiatrists had allowed him to leave the
clinic where he'd been locked up for a year. He would be able
to start to live again. It was in this room that he died, nine
months later.

He immediately made this new theater his own. And during
those nine months—a gestation period—he invented a new
role for himself. He had been the Patient, now he was the Doctor; he had been the Madman, now he was the Sage. He started
reading again—not novels, but essays, St. Thomas Aquinas and
Hannah Arendt, Jung and Plotinus (it's neurotics who read
novels, I was told shortly after his death by a psychiatrist I'd
met, psychotics prefer poetry and philosophy, they dig deeper
into reality). There, in his white room, he imagined himself a
thinker, a scholar monk; he was the isolated, banished Abelard
or a Renaissance melancholic seated at his writing desk, surrounded by books, globes, vanities, and tarnished mirrors. This
piece that he wrote then is not the story of his life but of his
illness. I don't know the identity of the *you* he addresses with

familiarity at the outset, the you who *knows*—another patient, a comrade, a soulmate? The man within him whom illness had left unvanquished and impassive? The *implacable Prosecutor* he had feared all his life, as he says, and whom he hoped to sway at last? Or a woman perhaps, a dream companion like those invented by unhappy children and lonely youths, a Heloise? He says, *Why do I not have a Heloise to whom I can write sometimes in my loneliness?*

He wanted to heal through this writing, and also no doubt to treat. A son and grandson of doctors, he had become a law professor. He wanted to die in his chair, on stage: *Like Molière, I should have liked to die in the midst of a class with my beloved students. God did not wish it so, if it be that he expressed himself through the psychiatric college.* He organized his writing like one of his classes, with the same attention to detail: two parts, each comprising three chapters split into sections. Here he kept all his fault lines and absences, his anxieties and ravings, in big *A*'s and small *b*'s. There's a crazy effort in this writing. I know who he was as he wrote it—exhausted body, failing heart, money problems, medication lists scotch taped to the bathroom mirror. I know what he had lost—furniture, apartment, job, the social identity that had meant so much to him, and those who had been close to him and turned away. Yet he presses no charges, there are no defendants, just an insane effort to see beyond the ruins inside him to the man whom illness had left intact, still capable of understanding, thinking, writing, and hoping. I can measure this hope by certain rearrangements, mismatches, or lies, the things his writing has already *novelized* (for example, he didn't live in *Montmartre, just below the Sacré-Cœur*, but much lower down, in a little street off the Rue des Martyrs, from where, it's true, you can see the Sacré-Cœur, but way above the rooftops. And in the notebooks he was writing in parallel—for himself alone this time—I read the dark pages, the pit every plan falls into, the fear of dying alone, the poison of the past, the absent future, the vanity of all novels.

There is still this writing. On the empty set, the vacant stage from which he himself is now absent, it's the last role he played. From where he's scattered—shadows or light, I know not which—he projects it still, black on white, these are his words, his voice, the smell of his tobacco, the uncertain, flickering light of a vanished star, the black sun of his melancholia. On the file that contains his manuscript he wrote, *To be novelized* and beside that a subtitle, which he later crossed out: *A Disturbing Specter.* That was what he called his illness. But perhaps he was also thinking of this writing, his bequest to my sister and me, and was afraid of burdening us with this most heavy of weights. The specter doesn't disturb me. It walks with me and I hold its hand, entwining its words through my own; in writing I lend it my breath, give it back its form. Through this book I keep it with me, anchoring it on my own shore.

Shortly after his death and when I already knew I would write about him (this book would have been written anyway, but while he was alive it would have been a black book, full of confessions and violence), he came to me in a dream, one of those dreams that are so dense, detailed, and frank that they are the sudden imposition of a presence. He sat massive, serious, and calm at the tiller of the old sailing boat he used to anchor in the Bay of Arcachon and, never taking his eyes from me, sailed away over a calm sea so pale it seemed to melt into the light of the sky. I rediscovered this dream later in a poem by Michaux—"Emportez-moi dans une caravelle, / Dans une vieille et douce caravelle, / Dans l'étrave, ou si l'on veut, dans l'écume, / Et perdez-moi, au loin, au loin." ["Carry me off in a caravel / In a gentle, old caravel / In the stem or even the foam / And lose me in the distance, the distance."]

You can't lose a father, particularly a father who was lost, or lost himself. It was perhaps while he was alive that we lost him, that we no longer knew who or where he was. Now that he's dead we gather up what he left, the crumbs and pebbles strewn through the forests of his anxiety, the treasure and the wreckage; we construct a void, we sculpt an absence, we seek out a form for what remains of him in us and has always been a temptation toward formlessness, a threat of chaos; we seek out words for what was always the secret, silent part in us, a body of words for a man who has no grave, a castle of presence to protect his absence.

Bond (James Bond)

My father wanted to be James Bond. Sometimes, when he wasn't well, he even was James Bond. At those times he would put on his pilot's goggles, slick back his hair, and, for example, dictate letters of application to the French intelligence services:

In August 1999, as my studies and exams were over, I dictated two letters of application to the internal and external intelligence services. One evening I drank a lot of wine and went to the police station to hand in my two letters. The results were unfortunate. I spent the night at the station etc., etc., and God's laughter reached my ears as the inspector in his fine uniform said, "It's funny for a former student to arrest his professor." And my thoughts turn to St. Thomas Aquinas, in whose view the drunkard takes ill-considered risks and encounters only trouble, whereas the temperate man considers and, if he acts, is surprised at how easy things are.

My father wanted to be James Bond because he wanted to be an *agent of the shadows: another project right for me: becoming an agent of the shadows, like slipping into a mousehole.* Becoming James Bond didn't mean being taller, stronger, more handsome, more conspicuous, skiing across glaciers under a hail of bullets from a helicopter galloping on a camel surrounded by a horde of Afghan rebels fighting an underwater battle with a harpoon against an army of frogmen driving a tank across Red Square with one hand while trying with the other to contain the screams of a brave but duplicitous young woman, no, becoming James Bond meant disappearing, slipping out of sight, going back to the rift within himself, hunkering down in its shelter. Becoming James Bond meant getting into a hole, like that night at the police station, but also becoming a mouse, changing scale and size, like Lewis Carroll's Alice when she fell down the well, becoming tiny, having the impunity of a child again, going around in a cowboy hat with a plastic gun and no one saying a thing, having the right to do anything, stupid things—what the French call *conneries* (of all the James Bonds his favorite was Sean Connery; before dictating his letters he had passed Connery in the street outside, *still very handsome, but a bit impotent* and *the old story* had *come back* to him).

Becoming James Bond also meant reconnecting with the old story, the family mythology. There were two heroes in the family. My father would talk about them, but there was always uncertainty in what he said, we never knew whether it was myth or history, novel or fact. One day, shortly after my grandfather's death, I went to Saint-Malo. My aunts had forbidden us—my father, my sister, and me—to attend the funeral. I had to think up a ritual, by myself and for the three of us, invent a ceremony, hear his name rise up during the mass for the dead, to the sailing ship hanging in the cathedral nave, check that it all existed, the *malouinière* chateau at Saint-Méloir, the house at Porte Saint-Vincent, reassure myself, perhaps, that—daughter of a black sheep and banished with him as I was—I could still retie the threads of lineage. On the morning of the day of the dead, I was walking at random through the deserted streets when, in the window of an antiques shop, I saw two books by my great-grandfather. The antiques dealer told me that he had only just put them on display. Of course I took this as a sign. I also realized my father hadn't been lying. There really was another story, which was not about family feuds, shame, and secrets, a story that merged with history, with splendors and glory. On the flyleaf of one of the books I discovered my great-grandfather's face. very *handsome* with a haughty chin, languid eyes, and the crimped hair of an American actor of the 1950s. He describes the siege of Saint-Malo by Allied troops, how he took in civilians and concealed men who were physically fit and wanted by the Germans in the shadowy cellars of the hospital where he was doctor-in-chief, how he performed operations under the bombardment while, imperturbable, my great-grandmother played bridge. So he was a hero, or almost, since, as an upper-class Catholic, he had thrown a few civilians onto the street to make way for nuns. His tone is dry and martial, with sudden emphasis in the last sentence: *I fled the Necropolis!!* The other family hero was truly heroic, an important member of the Resistance, Commander Joseph Pouliquen, founder of the Normandie-Niemen squadron and head of an army of shadows. My father called him Jo and regularly went to see him at the veterans' retirement home in Les Invalides.

A year after my father's death, I decided to have his strong-box opened. He'd told me about it one day, on the phone, from the little town in Picardy (far from Brittany, from the sea, from Paris too, his children and his work) where he was born and to which he had retreated to let go, to fall (he used to say it was his *falling point*). At that time, as I later realized, he understood that he was ruined. He had gone through his inheritance and run up debts, he was spending his university salary buying rounds for barflies, being robbed by unscrupulous friends, in short he might have said to himself that day, in a flash of realization, that he would have nothing to leave us, and he was trying to reassure himself. I listened to him with half an ear, it wasn't something I wanted to talk about, but he kept on, there's the Mercedes I bought from the Bulgarian ambassador, and that strongbox, things of great value, promise you won't forget, and he dictated the address and phone number of a Paris bank, made me note them down. So one day I decided to call them. The woman who answered remembered him, and I thought I heard a note of sadness in her voice, perhaps even respect, something very dif-ferent at any rate from the embarrassment and scorn I sensed in all the people I was dealing with at that time. The strongbox existed, he hadn't made it up, but the key was lost, it would have to be broken open. I was very late for my meeting with the locksmith, it's a habit of mine, but in that case, really and truly, I didn't want to go, I didn't know what I would find in that strongbox, most probably nothing, in fact I hadn't even thought to take a bag with me, I had a very clear impression of an act

of violence, a profanation, and in my head the phrase *a skel-
eton in the closet.* The locksmith was waiting for me, annoyed,
and together we went down to the small, dark, muffled room
where they keep the boxes, he sat me down and took a drill and
a crowbar out of his bag, I said he'd make a good burglar, that
we could be partners, he pretended to find that funny, he ranted
and cursed, went to incredible lengths, it went on and on, at
last the door gave way, he stood aside and solemnly asked me
to check the contents. The safe wasn't empty. It contained my
great-grandfather's gold watch, a little chain that had belonged
to my grandmother, an old edition of Montesquieu's *The Spirit
of the Laws*, a history book on the Normandie-Niemen squadron, an issue of *Icare*, "Journal of French Aviation," illustrated
with many photos of Jo Pouliquen, and, in a red leather case
bearing the Cartier monogram, some carnival decorations. So
it was that I broke into my father's imagination. He had told
the truth—the bric-a-brac that the bank employee rather apolo-
getically watched me pile into the plastic bag she had found for
me was beyond price. The keyless safe had contained a man's
memory, vocation, and dreams of glory, the material manifesta-
tion of a soul, the fetishes it would have chosen for its tomb, had
it had one, to accompany it into the other world, to take on the
army of shadows.

For my father James Bond was also a sort of scout, but of
a very particular kind, because what he warned of was the
enemy within. It was for this reason that, of all the inhabitants
of his personal bestiary, he associated Bond primarily with the
black sheep: *James Bond always lying in wait and the black
sheep grazing in the pastures nearby.* He envisioned this James
Bond—his inner agent of shadow—scaled down, a bit like a

Jiminy Cricket of consciencelessness, a little flying creature perching in the fault line into which his relationship with reality would plunge:

One night between Saturday and Sunday I saw myself lying where I was and James Bond, like a bird that had gotten into a house by accident, was flying around the bedroom banging into the walls, looking for a way out. Then, having tired himself, he perched in a corner above my head by the window that was still closed. This dream woke me up, which is unusual for me, and I went back to sleep feeling as though I were locked up. But peacefully. All week I kept James Bond inside me without thinking about him, walking calmly to the university like a good "Christian doctor" as St. Thomas would say, looking for his reunion with reality.

Shortly after this dream my father went to Morocco, where he had been sent as a legal advisor. King Hassan II died while he was in Rabat. He remembered having to leave his hotel, *requisitioned for the special services of other states,* going back to Casablanca, where a flight home awaited him, meeting a beautiful young guide, whom he followed into the desert as far as Essaouira, then nothing, the whiteness and light of the desert and, on one page of his journal, just the words, *I'm happy here . . . the King is dying.* For my part I remember that he came back from that trip in love, voluble, incoherent, talking about this woman who was waiting for him in the desert and whom he was going to marry, her brothers who had initiated him into Islam and were threatening him, and he gave my sister and me finely carved silver jewelry, chosen, he said, by his fiancée.

Another time I remember, it was summer, I was on holiday on the Île de Ré, pregnant with my first daughter, and he was in a clinic outside Paris. At least I thought he was, until he called me one evening. I could hardly hear what he was saying, we kept being cut off. He started by telling me not to worry, which was always a bad sign, then that he was in Normandy, staying at the house of some friends and in good company, because he planned to go to the Middle East, where Yasser Arafat needed him. He hung up. I called the clinic and asked to speak to the psychiatrist in charge of his case. She said that yes, he had gone out everything was fine I must have misunderstood, before advising me, with suspicion and a hint of aggression, to calm down. His manuscript puts it like this:

Certainly the clinic was lovely, the rooms spacious, the meals excellent. The doctors there were engaged in an extraordinary competition to outdo each other in elegance, I saw few of them and for a short time each visit. I spent my days reading Rimbaud and telephoned my father to read him excerpts, hoping to distract him in his widowhood. I was already losing my mind. I would dress as a cowboy, I had forgotten where I was, I was living a film or a lovely dream. The doctor would come to see me every day, he found it entertaining, we would talk about Jung. The great black hole was beginning, the downward spiral. All I remember is being given a place to stay in Normandy, buying myself miniature tanks, sketching out the creation of a huge consultancy company.

I am reassured to read these words. For the memory I have of each episode of his insanity is opaque, chaotic, as though I

were the one insane. Now I know we really did go through all
that together, even if he remembered it as a *lovely dream* and
I as a nightmare.

No one ever named his illness. Even after I grew up, when
the books I was reading and the people I was seeing could have
told me what it was called, I never tried to find out. Around me
they just used to say, "Your father's not very well at the moment." And my sister and I, though we used to talk about him
all the time, swap news about him, tell each other what he'd
said in his recent calls, we too never went any further: "Dad's
OK," or "not too bad," or "not well at all just now." I don't know
when I thought, for the first time, "My dad is mad," when I
adopted the word *madness*, that emphatic, vague, disturbing,
and slightly thrilling word, which named nothing, in reality,
except my anxiety, my childish terror, the panic I tipped into
with him and that my entire adult life was striving to cover
over. One call from him and everything—the garden, the summer evening, the nearby sea—would shatter, leaving me alone
with him in a fragmented, silent world that was perhaps reality itself (the day after his call I fell off my bike and spent the
rest of the holiday seeing doctors to reassure myself that the
child I was carrying was still alive).

Yet one day he saved me. It was in 1989 at the airport in
Sofia. I was coming back from a week's holiday with friends
and as I hadn't spent enough Bulgarian currency they stopped
me at customs. Before I left, my father had given me the phone
number of one of his former students, who was working at
the embassy. I called him and a few minutes later there he
was, a slightly timid young man who, for this occasion, arrived
nonetheless in dark glasses and an official car (perhaps the

same Mercedes that my father later bought and which was
to become an object of panic for him). He negotiated with the
customs officers and I was able to board my plane. My father
doesn't tell this story, but he liked to remind me of it. That
day he was, by delegation, a savior father, a hero father—or
perhaps ultimately just a father.

That's another thing I don't know about, something I can't
share in: I'm past the age of dreaming of a hero father (any kind
of hero come to that, great poet, great member of the Resistance, or a character from the films he used to take us to see on
Sunday afternoons at the Odeon—James Bond, Indiana Jones,
Luke Skywalker). In fact I don't think I ever was that age. And it
was many long years before I could even try to imagine what it
might be like to have a "normal" father. Actually it's an exercise
I've tried only once or twice, by dint of great effort, and with
disastrous results resembling some kind of advertising image,
but insistent and very clear: a mature man with a tan and salt-
and-pepper hair, sitting in his garden on a summer evening
with—out of shot but within reach—a wife, a dog, and some
gardening tools. This man is nothing like my father. He is tall, fit,
and slim, with steady blue eyes. I don't think I've ever met him.
I think I put this cliché together from aural images, from the
mix of assurance and childishness in the voices of daughters-
with-a-father (or, worse still, who write about their fathers).
But the hardest, most interesting thing was to try to capture
the effect: the world around this image was toned, rearranged,
criss-crossed with clear, straight paths, and I had the sharp, if
fleeting, sense that I could go down those paths, that I too could
be straight, firm, and grounded, unworried and incurious,
ignorant of margins and diversions, radiant and blinkered.

I've had a father. That father was neither a hero—though all his life he fought the shadow within him—nor an ordinary man. But he has bequeathed to me a heroic world, an infinite, labile, opaque, and teeming world, full of pitfalls and side-lines, hard shoulders and vanishing points—monsters too, and more or less amenable ghosts—and, with this world, the desire to walk through and describe it.

C

Clown

I'm five or six, on holiday with my father at his parents' place in
Soissons. My grandfather is seeing patients in his surgery at the
end of the garden, my grandmother is busy doing I don't know
what, I'm alone, I'm bored. Suddenly I have an idea. I get my
grandmother's lipstick from the bathroom and I set about paint-
ing my father: two circles on his cheeks, another on the end of his
nose. I take him by the hand and say, "You're a clown, Dad, come
on, I want to show everyone." Together we go out into the street
and sit down on the doorstep in the blazing sunlight of a summer
afternoon. He's in profile. With my finger I spread the color over
his left cheek. He lets me do it with a weary, nasty smile. Seeing him like this I'm filled with shame, sorrow, and pleasure. My
grandmother suddenly appears from nowhere, a small, elegant,
measured woman, her dress, makeup, and hair always just so.
For the first time I hear her raise her voice. In a tone that brooks
no answer she orders me to stop it at once, to go back inside.

Twenty-five years later, when my grandmother was long dead, my father went back to live, or rather to stop living, in Soissons. He moved into an apartment with his father. After my grandfather's departure and subsequent death a few months later, my father was hospitalized in a clinic right opposite the house he grew up in. It was then that he really went downhill.

I would take taxis so I would not see the surroundings on my own, I would buy drinks for barflies in exchange for a few words, I was waiting for I know not who, I know not what, at a table in the sun outside a café. I had lost my identity (and my papers too). The law that means so much to me was not enough to restore me to citizenship. I was "out of laws." I would sit outside the law courts where I had once been a trainee. One day I bought a broom and swept the courthouse steps. Every age has its pleasures they say. And the unconscious pleasure of playing the clown in the town where my father had forged his career manifested my sadness (they also say that clowns are sad). It gave me no pleasure to play that clown and I do not think there is any social code linked to the sorrow that drives you mad.

My father liked to kid around, he liked stupid jokes and word play: "A horse meets St. Thomas on his path and swallows him whole. Christ passes by and says, 'Laisse Thomas dans l'étalon.'* Isn't that silly?" and he would burst into delighted laughter. He didn't like tragedy. He also had a real talent for mimicry: he could put on any accent amazingly well and do animal calls too.

---

*Literally, "Leave Thomas inside the stallion," but it sounds like "L'estomac dans les talons," meaning "ravenously hungry."—Trans.

From this I deduce that he used to make me laugh as a child.
I can still see him, already very ill, playing with my daughter
when she was a baby and laughing with her, his laugh the same
as hers, effortlessly, no distance between them, without that air
of constraint, the bending down of adults acting like children,
as though she had awoken within him an element of comical
chaos and mindlessness that was very much alive and wanted.
He was fond of gaffes. One day in court he presented an important case with a clothes hanger hooked onto the back of his
robe. He liked nothing more than these involuntary deviations
and permissible skids that cause the social order, of which he
was otherwise so careful, to jam. At the end of his life, in the
little white room, he imagined himself as a wise monk, a man
of the shadows, and also as a clown:

*My little girl went to the circus on Sunday and I thought, "Why
not a clown?" It is not socially unacceptable. In a lovely little
caravan, going from town to town, making children laugh
and sleeping till the next day. But it is a fantasy, I know, even
though, before, I used to keep a clown's nose in a drawer in my
chambers. If a client had come in and told me stories, I would
have put on my nose and asked, "Do you take me for a clown?"
I never did it. You lose your clients and destroy your reputation
with such behavior.*

That clown's nose in his drawer, that jack-in-a-box, was his
violent desire to reverse roles and overturn codes, to mock
dignity. But he kept it hidden away, shut up in his drawer and,
costumed in gray, he would act the lawyer, deal with his dos-
siers, receive his clients, corseted by his reputation to protect,

his rank to retain. He played his role, he adopted the ways of
being and speaking of those around him, jurists, senators,
men of power, all ponderous with importance, pickled in arrogance. In so doing he used the same talent, the same flexibil-
ity—that inconstancy that Aristotle describes as characteristic
of the melancholic—that he used, when I was a child, to mimic
the call of a cow or pig. Often, in his voice, on his face, I would
catch the intonation or grin of a right-wing politician, seen on
television the day before. But it wasn't simply to be expected, it
wasn't just him. There was a wavering, a distance, an incredulity. He played the role but did not inhabit it. He acted the man
of law, but he was *out of laws*. In his family they didn't play
with codes. Nor did they worry about justifying them. They
were bourgeois without hatred of the proletariat, Catholic
without faith, affluent without greed, educated without curios-
ity. The main thing was to save face, or rather surface (the
gleaming furniture in my grandmother's house, the large mirrors that reflected her beautiful face, the polished apartment
in the 7th arrondissement of Paris, where she later gave refuge
to her son's distress). In psychiatry there's an illness they call
the *as if* syndrome. Sufferers act *as if* they weren't ill, *as if* everything were normal, *as if* something like normality existed.
This *as if* syndrome is, in a way, the illness of the bourgeoisie.
At any rate it was the illness of my paternal family, and that
of the parents of Fritz Zorn (I discovered *Mars* in my grandfather's library). Zorn died of cancer, my father of melancholia;
but sometimes I think he died of not having the *as if* syndrome,
of not having known how—or of being unable—to pretend all
the time, to act *as if* everything were fine, *as if* everything were
simple, *as if* what Zorn calls the "complicated" (sex, politics,

religion, ideas, and also the dark, opulent upheavals in which a person is forged, a life decided) had to be rejected, always, silently, prudently. Perhaps that clown's nose, had he worn it, might have saved him.

One summer—I might have been seven or eight, my sister three or four—he rented a caravan, a rickety old thing made of wood with a tarpaulin cover, pulled by a mare known as Cuddles, a real old gypsy caravan. We set off on a trip somewhere, in the Cévennes I think it was. We made our way very slowly along little mountain roads lined with meadows and forests and in the evening we would stop at an inn, let the mare out to grass, and the next morning, in the clear, clean air, we would set off again, my sister and I perched on the driver's seat in our flared dungarees and multicolored smocks, eating ice cream and singing at the tops of our voices, songs he'd taught us by Brel and Brassens, he'd be down on the road ahead, walking in front of the mare with a bucket of water or a bit of hay to keep her moving forward, laughing with us whenever she stopped. It was the end of the 1970s, he was young and slim, he had a moustache and a denim jacket, in fact I wonder if he didn't bring his guitar along. What I remember is that throughout that week everything went well, and my uneasy joy, and my disbelief.

Perhaps that was what he needed—to weigh anchor, cast off, leave watching eyes behind, and take to the road, alone but for a lazy old mare and two scruffy, giggling little girls. And yet his mask mattered to him, maybe it was he who held it in place. When I learned that the Latin for mask is *persona*, I immediately thought of him. For a moment I felt I understood his concern with codes, order, and hierarchy. The reason he wore himself out so much acting the adult was perhaps that, beneath his mask, there was no one, and that "no one" was not the saving, cunning anonymity of Ulysses, but emptiness, a gap. If he had dropped the mask we might perhaps have realized that *the king has no clothes*.

I did see my father like that, stripped, dethroned, fallen, my father become *nothing and nothing but nothing*, my father *drained of the abscess of being someone*. It was in the last years, during his last stay in a mental hospital—a real hospital this time, not one of those three-star clinics where exhausted teachers would go before summer to get treatment for incipient depression. Out of the question there to sit down at a café table in the sun or take a taxi ride around the local area. He was in what they call a "secure unit." To see him we had to go to a door with a small frosted-glass window and ring the bell. Then we had to wait for the nurse behind the counter to identify us, my sister and me. We would hear the electronic lock click and we would step into a room full of sickly colors— creamy white and chlorophyll green—where patients in slippers would slide silently toward the television through a cloud of smoke. All eyes would turn toward us, two girls wearing the air of outside, of life, of health, like an indiscreet perfume. I would avoid meeting their glances (but one day I recognized a boy I'd been at school with, tall, thin, and dark-haired, with a childlike face and glasses. I nodded to him, he didn't respond. Later my father told me he had recognized me too and that he hadn't wanted to talk about it). I was ashamed, ashamed of our appearance of health and normality, of our clothes, though we had chosen them to do him honor, to please him, perhaps also to show him that we were fine, that we were coping, and to protect us from all that, the dirty walls, the grim suburb, the pajamas and slippers. We were both very thin and silent, our faces drawn, clinging to our cigarettes just like the patients, but I found us noisy, arrogant, and overwhelming. My father wasn't in the day room. He was the patient in the room at the end. A lively, chubby nurse took us down to him. He was standing in a bare room with windows overlooking the garden and, in the distance, the Seine. My first thought when we went in was to open them, but they were locked shut. No mirror, no photos, no books or flowers. In a corner, piled up, the newspapers my mother had subscribed him to, still in their polythene wrapping. He was standing by his bed, dressed in a black turtleneck and gray flannel trousers that hung from his hips, with bare feet. They had confiscated his belt, the way they do with prisoners. For years we had seen him fat, swollen up by medication. He was thin, frighteningly so, he had almost disappeared. He seemed smaller too. We looked at each other, and what was in his eyes wasn't fear, or distress, it wasn't even nothing. It was absolute nakedness.

D

Departed

When my father died, he had already been gone a long time. He had long planned his departure, *deprived his family of himself.* For a long time already voices had always been lowered.

So I come to suicide, sin of the coward, who deprives his family of himself. In the first phase I had all my writings taken to the university library, so they could remain there as posthumous traces of me. In the second phase I squandered my little inheritance, quickly and without enjoyment, so much so that I afterward lived in debt. Then I stopped my teaching at a major business school, my lectures at the École Nationale d'Administration, and so on. It sometimes happened that I spent part of the night on a park bench, not drunk, but escaping the apartment and my office. I would also walk down the middle of the road to get myself run over. I would go and look at the Seine at night to throw myself into it. I would wander through

*the riskier areas of the capital. So it came about that—details
aside—an ambulance took me one day to a psychiatric clinic
in the town of my childhood. One August night I undressed and
threw myself into the water, seeking death in its eddies. Death
did not come. Disappointed, I returned to the bank, where the
barges were, and a helping hand pulled me out of the water.*

Yet we lived through all those years, my sister and I. There
were men to love, countries to explore, children to have, books
to write. My father departed from solid ground at a time when
my adult life was just beginning. He stayed with me just long
enough to witness its choices. I came back from England,
where I'd lived for several years, and suddenly encountered a
father, of a kind I hadn't known since I was a very small child.
He was no longer living with his parents, he and his girlfriend
had moved into an apartment—a little dark, a little sad, but
stylishly decorated—in Rue Notre-Dame-des-Champs, just
around the corner from me. He was working. In short, my
father was making a life for himself, my father was settling
down, my father was establishing his independence, I didn't
have to worry about him anymore, it was my turn now to do
all those things. Now I would be able perhaps to stop living between several men, several countries, to come home and stay.
We would meet for lunch at Le Rostand, near the Luxembourg
Gardens, the place where, throughout my entire adolescence,
I had seen him all puffy, exhausted, and neglected, with dirty
hair and sallow skin, clumsily eating a sandwich washed
down with a glass of Coca-Cola, staining his clothes, breaking
his silence only to tell me, thickly, of his anxieties, his difficul-
ties. And suddenly here I was, looking at a mature, elegant

man, a man who was sure of himself, who told me about his
Uruguayan partner, their weekends on the coast at La Baule
and Dinard, whose very self-centeredness gave me joy. Now
suddenly he was the one who wanted to know how I was getting on, so much so that, of course, didn't know—still don't
actually, but now, when everything gets too muddled, I can
revive the memory of his eyes and voice, laid down back then,
and a question he asked me, just one, that called for a precise
account of what I was, what I wanted and the shape I needed
to give my life. When I said "my father" that year, the words
held good—I don't know how else to put it—I had the impression of speaking the same language as other people, of living
in the same world (whereas normally, when I spoke those
two words, I would see an unbridgeable gulf open up between
what they evoked in others—the representation they would
create based on the image I was striving so hard to project, as
smooth and innocent and transparent as possible, precisely
in the hope of covering over that unbridgeable gulf—between
other people's words and my own private language: "my fa
ther," in other words my delirium, my distress, my demented,
different, deceased, departed father).

One day when we were sitting at a table outside Le Rostand, a boy I knew slightly, the son of a famous author, a
man successful with work and women, sat down at the next
table. My father greeted him with a smile, then got up to go
and deliver his lecture at the Sorbonne. "Who's that?" asked
my friend, then, "Your father? Really?" I immediately thought
he's surprised because I'm blonde and my father is very dark
because he has olive skin because I don't look like him, and
I changed the subject (smooth, transparent, innocent, make

other people talk, talk like the others so as not to talk about me). I did the same as the boy I'd seen in the mental hospital— I did my utmost to plug the gap between the ordinary world and the secret world I lived in with my father.

That year, the year my father came back to earth, we went on holiday together for the first time in a long time (ten years earlier he'd taken my sister and me to the little Spanish port where, as a teenager, he'd spent glorious summers swimming in deserted creeks and dancing barefoot on the beach. The little port had turned into one big concrete block, cluttered and noisy. We stayed in a building under construction far from the sea, my sister spent the time in bed with earache while, in the next room, my father and his partner of those days, a crabby, blonde dermatologist from Bordeaux, pointy-nosed and thick-hipped, steadfastly argued and I read Chateaubriand's *Memoirs from Beyond the Grave*, perched on cinder blocks so I could glimpse the sea. Never again, we had sworn, my sister and I). We went to Belle-Île in May. There a house awaited us, an old house surrounded by a huge garden planted with hydrangeas and rosebushes sloping down to a river mouth. The sun poured in through the bay windows. I would go down, very early in the morning, to swim in the cold water, I went for cycle rides along coast roads scented with salt and honey, I would lie on the heath amid samphire and orpine, in the evening we would have dinner by the harbor. I may well have seen my father, during that week, slender, smiling, and calm, sitting in the garden among the hydrangeas and rosebushes, by his side his Uruguayan partner, another blonde doctor, but whimsical and full of laughter, and their dog, a golden retriever that was a little crazy, which they would take to see a canine psychologist who cost a fortune but it didn't matter because only the dog was mad, everything was fine.

Then my father lost his mother, he and his partner went to live with his father in the polished little apartment on Rue de Grenelle, the laughing, blonde Uruguayan left in her turn, and the dog along with her, my father met another woman, even blonder and prettier, even madder. She was the mother of two little girls, born three years apart, like my sister and me. I often tell them about you, my father would say, and you know they're so funny, they play at having the same names as you two. One day I called him at his new girlfriend's place (I'd just found out I was pregnant with my first daughter) and the elder of the girls answered. I told her my name, or rather my nickname, the one my father chose for me when I was a baby: I'm Lou, who are you? I'm Lou, she replied, and my sister is Lili (that was what we called my sister). Shortly afterward my father announced he was planning to adopt them. A few weeks after that he was in the hospital.

And yet we lived through all those years, my sister and I, God knows how, hobbling along, tangentially. I had a little girl, I went on teaching my classes when he was unable to go on with his, I moved into a big apartment full of books and light while he went, suitcase in hand, from one clinic to the next, I published novels, wrote, as he did, every morning. A few scenes from those years come back to me, chaotically: the October day he decided to start teaching again, we had lunch together and, at the end of the meal, in a panic, he realized he'd lost his wallet, I calmed him down, went with him to the university, kissed him, left him, a few minutes later, worried, I turned back and ran to the Panthéon, wandered through the corridors looking for the room where his class was held until someone said no, he hadn't come in, no one had seen him; the winter evening, very late, when the phone rang, I picked up, baby in my arms, on the other end a psychiatrist told me he was with my father, that I had to stop him going out, drinking, going off, otherwise he couldn't answer for what might happen; the day I confessed to my mother that I couldn't take any more, I wasn't coping, I didn't know how to go on with all this, or the day when my grandfather told me, shortly before he died, that I should start thinking about myself, that there was nothing more I could do for my father. And so life went on, the adult life he'd helped me embark on, at the price of what forgetting I don't know, of what defenses and what burden I can't judge, the same, perhaps, as any life involves just to keep going, the same brutal obstinacy that everyone calls on to walk without stopping past a tramp stretched out on the street, to get on with works and days as soon as they close the newspaper, with the difference that, for me, misfortune, decline, and fear were infinitely close, no need to make an effort to imagine them, it was the rest that seemed abstract to me, the surface I too had learned to save, so much energy expended to seem smooth, normal, standard, to mask the chaos and keep my silent secret, to the point where, as I knew, my performance (like his before) was a little forced, I was afraid, always (picking up the children from school, at dinner parties), of betraying myself, the adult life I was working to weave hung on me like a flimsy, filmy garment, anything could have torn it. Only the baby reassured me, her awareness, I wanted to believe, went no further than the island where we snuggled together, and in her eyes I myself was no more than a presence without depth or history or childhood.

And yet, wherever I went, part of me lived in the shadows with him. I wrote, during those years, a novel about prison. I received letters from prisoners asking me where I'd done my time and also, one evening, a call from him: "You know," he said, "I've found lots of things I know about in what you write." After his death I opened the copy I'd signed for him. Below the final sentence, "Pierre bloody star around your head," he had written, in a rage, in biro, "NO!"

The last time I saw him alive, it was in a little restaurant near the Père Lachaise Cemetery on a cloudy day in February. My daughter wanted to visit the grave of her other grandfather, who had died a year earlier. I was tired that day, irritated by the child's noisiness, anxious at the thought of this encounter between her and her dead grandfather, annoyed also because my father, yet again, didn't have the money to pay for his lunch, because, yet again, he talked only about himself, because I felt as though I was looking after two children. I listened distract edly to what he said, his health problems, his senseless proj- ects (to become a professional letter writer, a psychoanalyst, a "coach," the word itself exasperated me, much more than the insane illusion it covered and which, in reality—but I couldn't allow myself the luxury of acknowledging it—upset me ter- ribly, because what my father had in mind, to make a bit of money and be useful, was to open a consulting room, to be- come, as he also said, "a good advice man" and offer lessons in life). Of him that day I have only a vague memory. I don't know whether he was wearing his raincoat or his big leather jacket, whether he had the hat and cane that made him look like a very old man. I remember he told me about a former model turned singer whom I knew slightly and he thought beautiful,

I sensed he'd said that to win me over but it just annoyed me all the more and I didn't even try to hide it. I spent my time getting up to go after my daughter, who kept running off to the kitchen or hiding under the nearby tables, I used it to do the same thing, to run away and hide. I couldn't make myself stay sitting there at the table with him, just be there, with him, he already seemed blurred by tiredness, annoyance, noise. Perhaps he thought, that day, that I would like him better dead than alive. He came with us through the cloudy, leaden day to the cemetery gates. At no time did I understand that we were in fact going there with him. I kissed him tenderly so as to be forgiven for my bad temper. I didn't watch him walk away.

E

Enfant [child]

It's a small, rectangular album, with torn leather binding and ragged corners. A watercolor on the cover shows a toddler in a sky-blue romper suit reaching out to a bush, which has poppies growing around it. Next to this, in big round, naïve letters, are the words "my son . . ." in the same blue. The black-and-white photos with lacy frames show a dark-haired baby, serious, looking down, taking his first steps in a clear sea, supported by a slender young woman in a flowery swimming costume whose hair, also very dark, is gathered in heavy tresses above her ears. Then the same baby, a little older, dressed in a kind of white burnoose, its hood hiding half his face, in a pram, sitting very straight, with a very dignified air and staring at the lens with stern eyebrows. On a beach in the South, dressed in a striped romper suit and the same little white hooded coat, the boy is on his feet, held up by frail thighs, smiling as he runs down a dune with a bucket in his hand.

Photograph after photograph, one per year or thereabouts: a
little boy in Vichy check shorts, squatting down with his older
sister in a makeshift tent and drinking from a bottle; holding
the paw of an Alsatian dog twice his size and laughing defi-
antly as he offers it a ball; driving all kinds of vehicles, from a
tiny boat on rockers to a sand airplane, a canoe he rows with
another child, another boat with a red sail that he steers alone
this time, sitting at the tiller with a victorious air, a stationary
motorbike by a sign that says *Prohibido el paso*, a black horse.
He has grown up. We've seen him in scout's uniform and just
before his First Communion, eighteen maybe, or nineteen, still
very dark, with short hair, and again dressed in white. Here he
is, cigarette between smiling lips, fencing extravagantly with
an umbrella and striking his tree-trunk opponent. He's acting
the clown, eyes half-closed, he is svelte, elegant, he looks like
a lighthearted, carefree, young bourgeois (as the photo was
taken at night, we can imagine him coming home from a party
with friends, a little tipsy, trying to make the girls laugh). The
next photo must date from the same day: he's wearing the same
trousers, the same white shirt, but he himself is not the same.
He is leaning back against a log wall, holding the umbrella
close, its handle against his neck. He's not smiling now, not
trying to entertain his audience. Head on one side, shoulders
stooped, he has a strange look in his eyes, a sideways, dark,
suspicious look, turned in on himself, frowning. On the same
evening, or the same night, a few hours later, he sits at a table
by the same log wall, harshly illuminated by a light hanging
from the ceiling. He's very handsome, his face a little hollow,
black, disheveled hair, with something distraught and bitter in
his pale eyes, the corner of his mouth. At his side can be seen

the blonde hair, perfectly defined eyebrows, and oval face of a woman who is not my mother.

And then nothing. Dozens of blank pages, some torn as though the images stuck onto them had been ripped out. Did they show my mother, their marriage, my sister and me as children? Yet at the end of the album I find once again the same photos of baby, beaches, and boats. I don't know who (he or his mother) tried to turn back the years, run the film backward, manufacture growth against time. But I do know that this unsettling arrangement expresses the truth of my father far better than the most faithful chronology could ever do. I find the echo of this in his writing:

Eternal five-year-old, a child at home, a hero to the outside world: this is a well-known duality and sometimes leads to manic-depressive psychosis.

My father was a five-year-old. My father was never older than five. In his writing he says it again and again, he's afraid it'll be forgotten:

Don't forget I'm five! (or five and a half)

He was five when he met my mother. She fell in love with him because he clowned around all the time and he was very good at roller-skating. I was born out of that, a love story between two children. I was already older than an eternal five-year-old when I first heard the story, so I regarded those two—the little blonde girl with dark, inexplicably slanting eyes, the little dark-haired boy proudly skating around the cathedral square—with

the amused superiority, the hint of pity felt by older children
for the younger. But also it felt as though childhood belonged
to them, as though it was entirely contained in this opening
scene, after mass one Sunday afternoon in a small town in
the provinces, the little girl with blonde tresses holding her
mother's hand, bored, while the local women swap the week's
gossip, and the little boy who suddenly appears, an excited,
dark-haired boy whizzing by on roller skates who executes an
abrupt turn, pulls a face, and the little girl, no longer bored,
bursts out laughing and, silently, stubbornly, decides she's going to marry him. Who would believe a story like that (and
yet I heard it from both, in agreement for once)? What room
is there, in this childhood vow, this crazy promise, for the rest
of life, the passing years, the childhood forever banished by
the children one has oneself produced? Fairy tales end when
children are born—they got married, had two children, and
the tale fell apart. The sullen little girl grew up, in her wedding
photos her eyes are still slanting and slightly somnolent, in the
molding of her cheeks, at the corners of her mouth she still
has some of the roundness, the vague torpor of childhood, but
here she is later with a baby in her arms, refined and alive,
chiseled into the delicate beauty of a Florentine virgin, awake
at last. He has not grown up. Nor has he betrayed anyone or
anything, but to what he has remained faithful I don't know.
To childhood, because it was the place where my mother and
he fell in love, or to my mother, because she was the preserved
pledge of childhood? Perhaps all he ever looked for, in those
half-closed eyes whose blackness had the vague, matte quality
of old mirrors, was the unsteady reflection of the little dark-
haired boy who, tall on his roller skates, felt king of the city,

master of his own destiny, who was panic-stricken when those eyes opened enough to see, next to his image, those of big cities, newborn children, and men who had better inducements than clowning to rouse them from their torpor.

Then he was the one who closed his eyes to the reflection, preferring to sleep, to dream. I have few memories from my childhood, fewer still from my childhood with them both (I was not yet five when they separated). I don't remember the things that gave shape to our days, the meals, holidays, good-night kisses, nursery rhymes, and stories, I have only the memory of a daily ritual, the way that, every morning, I would wake him by running a brush through his hair. This is also the only scene from my early childhood and the brief period when we lived together that he also describes:

When I took my elder daughter to school, she would wake me up with a hairbrush, brushing my hair, and then . . . and then . . . one day I heard my wife burst into my room, opening the shutters with a clatter, saying, "Get up! It's like living with an invalid!"

After that it was the law of silence within me.

Among the photos in the little beige leather album, there's one I find particularly touching, or rather more familiar than all the others (the images of the dark-haired baby have something anonymous about them, the pale distance of all family albums; the melancholic young man, meanwhile, is someone I know, I recognize him, but by that in him that has always been foreign to me). It's a photo taken in the morning, when he has just woken up. Wearing striped pajamas, in bed, resting on his elbow, he's reading a comic book. His sheets and cheek are splashed with sunlight and there's no way of knowing whether it's this light or the vestiges of sleep that make him screw up his eyes and wrinkle his nose. He's not posing, not looking at the lens, he almost certainly hasn't even noticed he's being photographed. He is there, fully there and at the same time withdrawn, absorbed in the great solitude and freedom of reading and sleep. He's twice his eternal age, ten or eleven, he is moving away from his childhood and toward that madness within him that refuses to leave it, and these stories go with him, the stories that, throughout his life, he never stopped telling. The adventures of Prince Eric, perhaps, who was part of a personal pantheon along with James Bond? As an adult, when all the powers of reality, of disappointment and betrayal had joined forces to dethrone him, he still dreamed he was a king's son:

Family tradition has it that the Comte de Chambord, pretender to the throne of France in 1875, conducted his campaign with some recourse to the coffers of my great-great-grandmother, a lawyer's widow, leaving by way of thanks a fireback and, who knows, perhaps a small black sheep . . . But this is an excessive presumption.

One horrible evening of loneliness I went to the chaplaincy of the diocese. And I said, "I am the descendant of the Comte de Chambord, I have come just to say an Our Father with you." Which I did, then left. Clearly I was not at all well.

No matter how much he invented royal genealogies for himself, drew multicolored trees whose abundantly forking branches bore the names of sailors, priests, men of the law, and doctors, and established the legitimate pretensions of his daughters to the throne of France, he was, throughout his life, more of a son than a father. When he went back to live in the small town where he had been boy-king, champion swimmer and roller-skater, umbrella fencer, adroit escort and entertainer of girls, he took his father with him. And when, shortly afterward, his father died, he became him: his hair turned white, he began to wear his father's clothes and hat and to carry his stick, passing without transition from the age of five to eighty-five.

I waited for my father, taking—excessively for me—the plea-sures I should have liked him to take in a sort of manifest tran-substantiation: I wore his coat, walked with his stick, etc.

At that time he had a brief encounter with death: his heart gave out for the first time, and it was a kind of rehearsal for the proper meeting, the big one. We found out, my sister and I, when we got a call from the police station. We went by train to see him in the hospital where, years before, his father had treated failing hearts while my mother's father was bringing children into the world. He was lying in the gray light, dressed in pale green social assistance pajamas, thin, exhausted, and determined to stop living. He had hardly woken up from his operation and already he was leaving his room to go and smoke in secret. We no longer had the strength for scolding and exhortations. We soothed and comforted him like a child. When we asked him, gently, why he had gone to live so far away from us, and he told us it was to get closer to his family, we reminded him that his father was dead, that he had cut his ties with his sisters, that we were his daughters. Later he told us that, with these words, something had revived within him. He postponed his death for another two years.

A large black-and-white portrait found among his papers shows a chubby little girl, blonde hair cut anyhow and held back with a barrette. She has the same mouth, same smile, same age as the very dark-haired little boy, the same eyes too, the same imploring trust, already veiled, in her case, by a wisp of knowledge, of forgiveness. He has stuck a yellow Post-it note on this photo with the words, in his handwriting: *To break a promise is to fail God (African proverb).* This little girl who was me is no more familiar to me than the child who smiled the same smile thirty years before. I couldn't name her pleasures, her sorrows, any more than his, or say what it was she'd already learned to fear and to hope. What I do know is that in having lost him I have lost her too. That woven obscurely through her was a knowledge that was taken away from her very early and was the presence beside her of this man, my father, the great shadow in whose company her life began. In both faces I see nothing but childhood, the same childhood, and expectation, the same expectation. And while there are many images I have learned to look at, others that I force myself, gingerly, to decode, I struggle to look into the eyes of the child who was my father; while there are many things that I try to understand, that I have learned to accept, I can't come to terms with the promise that was irreparably broken, with what this child lacked, with that which forever failed to meet his expectations, his great, silent, trusting expectations, and so I too would like to arrange the images in reverse order, eradicate the double space of our unsynchronized lives, find in his

death what it is that abolishes time, pass through death to find
the child, to meet that boy with desperately trusting eyes, to
stay with him, to protect him.

F

Flic [cop]

He had such a love of order and ritual, finery and ceremony, he had played so often with his own death, that I was convinced, when it came, that he must have tried to give it a form, to shape it in his own image and that of the life it had penetrated so deeply. In the little white room I opened boxes and files, flicked through his countless notebooks for the first time, found the blue folder and the manuscript it contained. And, on page 169, I read the words that gave his death a face:

I'm hoping for a pretty death: cremation, a memorial mass with perhaps a few pieces of music, an extract from Dies Irae to beg forgiveness for my furious rages, another from De Profundis so that my life in the hereafter—with the resurrection of the body—will spare me the melancholia that has made my time on earth so tempestuous. And then my ashes scattered by night around the ~~church of St. Étienne-du-Mont~~ nearest church, at the

entrance to my university, keeping a few back, if possible, for the
Luxembourg Gardens, by the Medici Fountain.

This was one promise we could keep. We just had to do as he
wrote in those few lines that I read and reread till I knew them
by heart. But as I strove to put them into practice, I discovered
traps and strange tangents. At his mother's funeral he had
asked the organist for a gentle Toccata, anything but Dies Irae.
To spare him (he had already paid enough for his rages and
passions), in my turn, I betrayed him. I asked the organist to
play Schubert's "Ave Maria" and *a gentle Toccata* (she played
me several, over the phone, from the church of St. Germain-
des-Prés. I was sitting in my office with my cell phone, the
great organ resounding, then suddenly I stopped her: that one.
After the ceremony one of his childhood friends told me that
back then he used to listen to it all the time, it was his favorite).

He spoke of the *resurrection of the body,* but his own body
he wanted to shed, very early, very radically. That's why he
thought of a *memorial mass.* This was, I discovered, the ex-
pression adopted by the Church, which denies a funeral to
dead believers who don't want to rot in the earth. He led us,
my sister and me, a merry, twisting dance of in-and-out, a
precise, premeditated game with dogma and rules. We were
obliged to adopt the conventions, which were those of his
caste, and besides part of him followed them keenly, but we
could only succeed by approaching them obliquely, with an
incomplete, reticent, uncomfortable adherence that sent us
back to the margins that we occupied with him and, beyond
the upheaval of his absence, maintained our fragile, tenacious
trio, our complicity.

The priest gave us the urn containing his ashes, asking us with sympathetic concern, as though speaking to followers of a different faith, if we knew what to do with them. At Père Lachaise I had been given a leaflet that, among other sordid, laughable recommendations (so unbearable I ended up wondering whether they might reflect some superior wisdom, a concern to render the whole thing acceptable—death, the charred body, and the pure insanity of a person contained in a tiny receptacle, the entire universe forced into a bottle by a mad model maker—by reducing it to the ordinary, authoritarian register of obedience to the law), stipulated that it was forbidden to scatter ashes in a public place. I understood then why my father had used the phrase *by night*, why too, worried more for the divine law he believed in than the human law he taught, he had crossed out the church of St. Étienne-du-Mont and written *the nearest church*. He knew about the ban, that was his job: but, even from death, he still found a way to transgress it.

He, the dead man, was the one we obeyed. Paris's Latin Quarter was under siege. Students were demonstrating against the introduction of a new kind of employment contract, the Sorbonne was closed up and fenced off, the streets were full of riot police. This chaotic frenzy, this brief disruption of the ordinary world helped me, carried me, and I was sure too that he wouldn't have been sorry to depart in that atmosphere.

We weren't brave enough to scatter his ashes *by night*. We devised scenarios, my sister and I, such as driving down Rue Soufflot at top speed on a scooter with the urn tied on the back, letting the ashes escape. In the end (I don't remember

how, I don't remember doing it, I went through it all in a kind
of stubborn daze) we put them into envelopes carried open
in our pockets and walked up Rue Soufflot in our mourning
clothes and the bright daylight of a spring afternoon, past the
cordons of riot police, smiling to divert their attention, and,
step by step, shaking our envelopes.

(The church of St. Étienne-du-Mont, where he had married
my mother, I don't know, I've forgotten that too, I only remember having gone around it several times with my envelope in
my hand, looking for a quiet corner, a deserted chapel, stunned
by all the light that was pouring in and the whiteness, the stiff
infallibility of the tombs of the important dead, which left no
place for mine, even if in the end I almost certainly, shamefully,
furtively, placed a pinch of ashes behind the high altar, where
Racine and Pascal also have no tombs, I don't know, I've forgotten. He rests in the Medici Fountain, where he used to meet
my mother, in the mossy little back basin, guarded by loving
couples and serious young people bent over books.)

He needed rules and laws so he could obey and break them, so
he could be punished, brought back into line, and so he could
apply them, he needed all that without knowing which side he
was on, cop or robber, the law at least didn't shift around, it
was his guardrail. In his wallet I found the card of the Friends
of the Police, which must have been sent to him in exchange
for a subscription. The photo shows him on a bad day, swollen, veiled eyes, baleful smile. But the left-hand corner of the
card has a stripe of blue, white, and red and I wonder if he
hadn't kept it, in the top slot of his cardholder, so that if neces-
sary he could show it, flash it quickly like in the films, like a

kid, so he could pass for a cop. He was haunted by the expectation of punishment. Near the end of his life, in the evening on
the phone, he would go on and on about his car, the Mercedes
bought from the Bulgarian ambassador. He was in such a state
of panic that in the end we did wonder, my sister and I, whether he had run a pedestrian over in a hit-and-run accident. He
told us he had simply lost his papers. I took him to the police
station to report them lost, holding his arm to make him keep
walking. He was convinced he would never come out again.

*I called the police station during my panic attacks. I remember
that when I told a young policeman I was scared he said he'd
send me a* "pas-trouille."* *That made me feel better.*

He liked decorations and corporations; to gather his pieces together he wanted a *constituted body.* For a time he belonged to an
order of Freemasons. I found his insignia and his blue and silver
apron. He called them his brothers, he had dreamed up a family.

*Where are the families of yesteryear? I knew what are called
very old families: the lineage of one included a young man who
was very sweet, but to whom the Virgin Mary appeared when
he went to the cinema . . . He lived for a long, long time in what
is still called the local asylum.*

One day he stopped acting as if, pretending. He accepted that
he was the black sheep of his family, the anomaly, gave up

---

*"Patrouille," meaning "patrol," sounds like "pas-trouille," meaning "no fear."
—Trans.

attuning (as he used to, back then, during those meals that still brought them together, when I was a teenager, him and his sisters, around a white tablecloth covered in silver, in houses outside Paris weighted down with gleaming furniture, thick curtains, where the lights stayed on even during the day, as though the light from outside was to be avoided at all costs, maintaining the fake lighting, the lying decency of bourgeois order beneath which were steeping poisons that, as the meal progressed, would rise to the surface—a love of money, the reduction of sexuality to obscenity, a hatred of foreigners. My father would remain silent or, sitting between his daughters, would act the child, returning to his place as the youngest, the longed-for only son, watched over with still tender indulgence, the last vestiges of complicit laughter, by his two sisters, my aunts who were once so beautiful in the photos from Spain, with their bare feet, white dresses, and loose hair, my aunts who adored going out, dancing, who had scandalous love lives, now corseted by their suits, pearls, and chignons. Then, over dessert, my father would get his breath back, fall into step with his brothers-in-law, taking his turn to toss in a racist joke, a smutty story, and I never knew which made me more uncomfortable, which I hated the most, the distressing jokes, his silence, or this fearful, desperate effort to make a show of allegiance, the ritual renewal of his membership. Afterward it would take many hours, long walks outside with the boy I'd returned to, for me to dispel my discomfort).

His sisters stopped receiving him, and then speaking to him. They let him stagger through the streets of the small town where they'd played together, shared friends, danced together at the same parties, shut themselves away in shame when a childhood friend told them she'd seen him in the street, dirty and drunk, when neighbors in their building confided that he'd asked them for money or something to eat, when the concierge started calling him "the madman" (*My concierge called me "El loco" (the madman) during my last episode, she should go and sweep up her own detritus!*), not to mention the terrible stories he would tell anyone willing to listen, how his father took refuge with his older sister after their falling-out and died alone in an old people's home, his brother-in-law stripping his mother of her jewelry on her death bed, sixty years of effort and there he was, blowing the whole lot apart, so that everything that they had carefully kept to one side, thrown down the trash chutes of their lives—poverty, debauchery, alcohol—everything they regarded as the essential qualities of those others, the scum, the homeless, Arabs and blacks, he brought it all bursting back into the bright light of day.

He, meanwhile, was waiting for forgiveness from them, or a curse, perhaps for consecration. He had passed to the other side, the side of all that centuries of bourgeois tradition had persistently swept under the carpet (though there had been that Breton grandmother of whom it was said that her head wasn't quite right and she was a little too fond of the bottle, but she lived with them when he was little, with no scandal or outbursts, or that baron cousin with a privateer's name, heir to the *malouinière* at Saint-Méloir, who one day confessed to my father that he, lord of the manor, title-bearing upholder of the family honor, suffered from the same sickness). He had passed to the side of chaos, had embraced that role directly, headlong, this time it was obvious, he was the cop turned robber, good turned bad, fine gentleman turned ragged tramp. Yet he kept

on trying to find a place on the family chessboard—king's jest-
er, idiot of the family, no matter, so long as he still belonged,
with a place to occupy, anything apart from emptiness, the
desert, definitive marginalization.

*In China "madmen" are thrown naked over the fence of an en-
closure for those of their kind, to whom food is thrown. In other
civilizations "madmen" who are not dangerous have their place
and function. Some peoples believe they drive away evil spirits.
That is the case in Africa. They have their place within the tribe
or family. In North African families, a "madman" is protected
by blood ties. Those who have suffered tragedy, or destabilizing
emotion, are always supported by their families. The extent to
which patients in institutions are supported by Arab families
has been observed in this regard.*

Yet it was on the margins that he created ties and found a tem-
porary family. Whenever we went to see him, my sister and
I, in the last hospital he spent time in, he did not greet the
other patients. Now he had the right to come and go as he
pleased, we would stay on the grounds chatting, under large
trees whose shadow was as cool as the Seine flowing nearby.
We would talk about the future, trying to sketch it out, to find
words that would give him back the desire for it, we would
talk about renaissances, lives that can start anew at any age,
the man we knew who, at the age of thirty, fell madly in love
with a pregnant woman he met on a train, lost touch with her,
got married, then, aged eighty, had just met up with her again,
a widowed grandmother now, and was going to marry her.
Sensing that it was derisory, absurd, we gave him advice—cut

your hair, do yoga classes, read novels—advice he would receive in silence, absently, and we would need to make a huge
effort not to fall with him into that silence, that absence, to
keep speaking to him in the vain, proud language of the living.
If a patient happened by, he would glance at him briefly with
a look full of fatherly pride, the desire to protect us, and a kind
of established connivance. One time we followed him into
the refectory to get ourselves Coca-Colas. The others were already sitting down, next to the Subbuteo and Ping-Pong tables,
under the neon glare. In the faces turned toward him there
was, above and beyond devastation, a tenderness, a respect, a
hint of envy too, and his attitude, his way of putting his arms
around us, walking faster while returning their glances, said,
I'm with them, don't touch, don't come near, but I'm still one
of you, I haven't forgotten you. And I felt then that something
was happening between them and him that was beyond us,
that operated at unsuspected depths of distress and humanity, and that, at least as much as from us, it was from them,
with whom he shared the same unspeakable secrets, the same
naked, shattered world, that he would draw the strength to get
better, to leave them.

*I remember the sunny terrace outside the last hospital, where
I realized that I could not blame God for the new destiny that
awaited me supported by my daughters. Some were truly alone,
like the poor fat bed-wetting woman who no longer knew how
many years she had spent under lock and key, the tall man
who had set fire to himself and whose face seemed melted, who
never had visitors and was always very affable, an old lady
dressed like a little girl with a straw hat from a Renoir paint-*

ing, a former dancer from the opera house who had become schizophrenic, not to mention all those little old men they call mad and who are condemned only by their social uselessness, and the homeless. In that hospital I had many, many conversations, speech having returned to me under the vault of magnificent trees.

G

Gisant [laid out]

My daughter's birthday party had just finished. The apartment was full of balloons, garlands, and children. One last little boy was still waiting for his parents, a little boy with long, curly, very dark hair. The telephone rang. I think it was already nightfall. The police were waiting for us outside my father's building. They didn't leave me alone with him. One of them preceded me into the room where he lay. He never took his eyes off me, told me not to touch a thing. I had to ask permission to kiss him, to take his hand. The inspector checked with my sister, seven months pregnant, that she had really been the one to find the body (it was indeed she who, worried that she hadn't heard from him, had gone to his place, rung the bell in vain, broken down the door with the concierge. I hadn't worried, I was expecting him over the next day to celebrate the birthday all over again). And to passersby and neighbors he replied that it was nothing. In the little white room, already

deep in shadow, my father was resting, lying on his narrow
bed, tucked in like a child, a lighted lamp beside him. For a
long time I sat there beside him, looking at all the objects that
surrounded him, watched by the suspicious eyes of the man
in uniform, I wanted to keep it all in my memory, record every detail, the pattern on the carpet, the papers on his desk,
the opened pack of cigarettes, the shadow and light on the
pictures, as though this décor that had been with him in life
and was witness to his death contained the secret of both, as
though remembering things were the guarantor of my fidelity.
Of him I no longer had, did not yet have a memory. It was only
when I leaned over to place a kiss on his forehead, still warm,
smooth, and calm, that the little girl inside me woke up, her
child's body quivered, and with it the very ancient, deep, silent, faithful imprint of this body beside it, these arms that had
carried her, cradled her, the shoulders against which she had
pressed her face, the hand that, at bedtime, would draw magical signs on her forehead to accompany her into sleep, to protect her from the night, this child's body, awoken in an instant,
was in an instant crushed, torn away, rooted out, along with
him who had given her life, leaving her, the adult, more empty
and hollow than a young woman who has just given birth. The
madness of death, of the body that remains, stranded, opaque-
ly, stubbornly present, a monumental stone inscribed with
signs now forever meaningless, madness of being torn apart
by presence and absence, and of the days that followed when
I sensed him lying there, worried and weighty, in a cold room
by the Seine, kept back on the bank, frustrated in his desire,
the great desire that had long been his, for nothingness, yes,
to that I would have preferred annihilation, the void striking

like lightning, a shipwreck with all hands, anything but this uncertain place, this chiaroscuro through which I wandered with him who was not quite dead while I was no longer really alive. It was many days before I was allowed to place, one radiant spring morning, beside this body lying under a sheet I'd been told not to lift, children's drawings, wooden sailing boats, a bunch of narcissi, and to trace in turn on his veiled forehead the magical signs that would accompany him into the night, to stay wailing, again, in a little room open to the river, in the company of Arab women wrapped in multicolored cloth and weeping for a son—a twin death—then, sitting beside him, to cross the city, the noisy, living city that I saw going by behind the tinted windows of the hearse, as if I were going to leave it forever, with him. Many days, years, for signs to regain their power and change absence into memory, shipwreck into treasure, to veil that opaque forehead, that body without grave or rest, in a shroud of words, for it to lie lightly upon him.

H

Hoffman (Dustin)

In profile the resemblance is staggering: raven-black hair, hooked nose, hollow cheeks, a thin, wiry outline, and also a kind of absence to the world, a buriedness in himself that's visible from the opening shots of *The Graduate*, when Benjamin glides along the airport travelator past big windows, on the edge of the void, when he flops, head back, into the airplane seat, wrapped in a shroud of light, in the fine, terrifying whiteness of beginnings,

a kind of distance, a gap, a refusal, the main thing being not to do as the others do, not to become like them, the noisy, faded adults, the open mouths that shout and snap at the air, not to go over to the other side, not to join the party, to stay behind the pane, looking at them like fish in an aquarium, through dark glasses or a diver's mask, diving into a silent, undulating world, into the wordless, monotonous pleasure of bodies, into white torpor, staying there on the bottom of the swimming pool, far from voices too loud and lights too bright, *in the sounds of silence*,

until at last comes the girl, the sister-lover Elaine, the one you can talk to for hours shielded from the others in a car with closed windows, the one for whom, at last, it's meaningful to feel alive, enough to cross bridges, rivers, anger and hate, and the blocked-up lives of adults like caged apes,

to be on the other side of a pane of glass one last time, crying out, and now she hears that cry, she answers, it's the others now, in their wedding clothes, who shout in silence, mouths open, prisoners of the church, its transparent walls locked with a cross, while together the two of them run and laugh,

now they're the ones being spied on—sitting at the back of the bus they don't see the others, their eyes don't meet, they look into themselves, stupefied and fearful, wrapped in white light,

will their life, the life now moving on, still have the innocence and glory of this escape,

looking at them—the dark-haired, wiry boy, the girl with kohl-blackened eyes and a childlike face—I think of my mother and him, the fragility of young love and first promises,

later I see him in another film—its title, *Kramer vs. Kramer*, intrigued me as a child—he's still as thin, hair longer, features more pronounced, the woman beside him has the sharp, worried blondeness of Meryl Streep and the music has gone, along with the vast whiteness and suspension bridges, instead there are corridors, kitchens, offices, and squares, the corners and clutter of adult life you find yourself in without really knowing how you got there,

I saw that film in Ivory Coast, some nuns were showing it to their class, I soon realized why, they saw it as grist to their

rosaries, the mother leaving her post, the horror of divorce
and women's liberation, but once again I thought of him—

*simply, and no one knew, I was hospitalized during the Christ-
mas holidays and in July. I felt ugly, swollen-faced, my clothes
were too tight, and with my children I was like a fat Dustin
Hoffman—I remember the botanical gardens, the children's
park with its "enchanted river": laughing with them before taking them back to their mother, still so beautiful*

—when she left, she took us with her to a small apartment,
its walls painted bright pink and violet, where her comrades
from May '68 and her feminist friends came and went, she was
coping well, he was cracking,

and yet, watching that film (that bad, sentimental, reac-
tionary film) in the stifling African night with nuns nodding
knowingly and little girls with braided hair wondering what
story it was that they were being told while around us insects
drawn to the electric light fell to the ground in a thick carpet of
gray wings, I couldn't help thinking of him,

thinking, looking at this father alone in an apartment with
his child, that he had done just that for us too, that he'd had
to do it, when we went to him for a weekend or for holidays,
keeping his ghosts and delusions at bay to perform the ac-
tions that cradle childhood, to find, from his dwindling store
of energy, enough to nurture our vulnerable, voracious lives,
to preserve an island of order amid the chaos he was in, time-
tables and rules in a reality that was crumbling away (giving us
baths in the tub in which, the rest of the week, he would wash
his shirts together with his dog, making our dinners, tracing

on our foreheads, at night, at bedtime, the magical signs that
protected us)—

*I have known no lasting happiness but that which comes from
the existence of my children, all the rest seems to me to be pre-
carious, fragile, threatened*

—I remembered what he said to me one day, a man you know
isn't afraid to have children, he's afraid of losing his children,
and suddenly I sensed, with suffocating strength, so that I immediately wanted to forget it, the loss with which we must
have left him.

L

Illuminated

In my father's manuscript, there are fifteen pages written by me. Or, more precisely, fifteen pages rewritten by him. They're in a chapter in the second part, entitled "Moral Inheritance." In it my father talks about a very ancient text, in Greek, a treatise by Plotinus, full of ellipses and impatient inquiry. The piece talks about the soul and the body—who's still interested in that?—the soul, which, because it merges its life with the body's, becomes blocked, darkens, and dies, in the way that souls die; the animal, which is that part of us that feels pain and pleasure; the pure pleasures of the impassive, impeccable soul; the self too, the ego, which Plotinus calls the "us" because, he says, "we are many," at once animal that feels pain and pleasure and impassive, changeless soul, at once god and animal. For years this piece was always with me. I made a translation of it, with a commentary, and, when this was published, I took it to the psychiatric hospital. Every time I visited

I saw it on his bedside table, among the novels he didn't read, the newspapers he never even opened. Then my father came out of the hospital, he started to get better, he began to read again:

Abelard was cured of his sorrow by his passion for study, I, thank God, have that passion poorly repressed, even though in times gone by I was no longer even thinking. Those passions feed thought and for the sick they dominate what is called rumination or what Jung describes as the circular oscillations of the manic-depressive.

Thus it was, on the other side, during my first weekend of free life, that I sensed the importance of morality. And it was like a black light bursting out of the boxes I opened as I rediscovered my books.

One evening on the phone he told me, "I'm reading your Plotinus, you know, it's fascinating, that's it exactly, we are many, it's true, we don't know who we are, even though, sometimes, in dreams, we meet them, our other selves."

This unquiet, elliptical, jerky piece of writing, shot through with distant beauties and ideas to which the keys have long been lost, this text read by no one I knew (they would thank me politely and shut it at once, overburdened), these eleven pages of shifting, tortuous Greek whose every word I had scrutinized in the grip of a fascination that, for fear of weakening it, I preferred not to formulate, for him too it carried a truth, the same, perhaps, as the one I sought within it—the crowd we each conceal and contain, the inability to grasp oneself, to coincide with oneself, the consciousness that dilutes and fragments, and those moments when we are taken out of—and feel at last that we belong to—ourselves, fully, silently, unthinkingly present to others and to the world. And I came to think that perhaps this truth was his, that this text had encrypted his own oscillations from angel to beast, joy to pain—each of them excessive—his inner multitude and his always escaped self, the exact formula of his melancholia. Here was a silent transmission from him to me or, who knows, from me to him, for (as I discovered reading his manuscript) he kept our kinship quiet, citing my name without ever referring to me as his daughter, calling me the *author* and, once, *my dear philosopher*, and presenting himself as the *heir* to this piece, as to the great, dead thinkers with whom he was in dialogue. This inversion and adoption of distance moved me deeply; it seemed to attest to a timeless complicity between him and me, unconnected to heredity.

According to her publisher, the author seeks to enter into the movement that leads from passions to thought, from pain to impassivity, the animal to the divine: this involves, she says, undergoing an "initiation." Here I see the theme of the inner conflagration that leads to bipolar disorder and its consequences. I know that the body and mind remember everything and that the demon Er is always lying in wait. Does soiling of the soul take as long to fade as that of the body?

Not only had he read the text, he too was commenting on it, translating it, filtering it through his own life and illness. He starts with a word-by-word commentary:

"To whom," asks Plotinus, "should we attribute pleasure and pain, fear and boldness, or suffering?" In relation to boldness,

first of all, we can recall certain characteristics of phases of elation, such as loss of inhibition and the acceleration of thought. At such times the tormented soul may take deadly risks. It behaves worse than the animal, because we do not see animals becoming dangerous to themselves and others. Where fears are concerned, depression is not characterized by anxiety, but I have known states of panic that made me flee—flee, walking drunkenly through the night unable to stop. As for the word pain, it sounds wrong to me, I have been on the receiving end of it too often and too regularly in psychiatric institutions, like the water dripping on the torture victim's head in China.

But he is critical of the text too. He doesn't want an impassive soul, doesn't believe in it, he's too familiar with the soul's sicknesses, clashes, and pains. An impeccable soul perhaps, at last removed from the fear of crime and punishment, the implacable Prosecutor, but impassive? What does that actually mean?

When I was 6 or 7 years old, one summer on the Costa Brava, I saw some former SS soldiers. They were members of the German legion that had come to give added force to Franco during the Civil War. They were recognizable by their scarred cheeks, the ritual marks of swordfights at the military academies. On those evenings my mother would dress in blue, white, and red. But they terrified me because of course these impeccable men had learned to be impassive in the face of other people's pain, which they had made their vocation.

He didn't want a soul that was indifferent to the sufferings of the animal. He speaks of compassion and the bestiary teeming within him, black sheep, silent sea fish, and nightmarish galloping, the *animal*, he writes, *is a springboard with which to rise to the height of the soul.* He also talks about the dog that would put an end to his ravings on the phone *by planting himself in front of the desk, then collapsing, stiff, on his side in a single movement, with a deep sigh,* or which, in his depressive phases, came and curled against his belly, *all the presence of his powerful body come to the aid of my unimpassive, fatally wounded soul, my soul gone bad perhaps? That being so I like him too much for my soul to be carried by him.*

What he likes in the text is its promise of elevation, a serene, luminous state in which, taken out of oneself—both noisy bestiary and shattered ego, agent of shadow and implacable prosecutor—one can share a little of the light he was starting to see, in his small white room, in his last months.

. . . *communion with the universal, something undefined and infinite, communion with the sky that, through clouds, can give us images, with the stars that wink at the man with a melancholic disorder, for, it is said, they contain lithium.*

J

In my father's theater of shadows, alongside the implacable Prosecutor sits a Jesuit Father: he has sharp eyes, a falsely good-humored air, he smokes a pipe, and beneath his cassock his feet are ice-cold. Every morning he breaks into his dreams to wake him up:

Whenever I awoke the Prosecutor within me would be waiting, or the Jesuit Father, I know not which, for his indictment the first, his work of fostering guilt the second. These moral assizes every morning, and on awakening from siestas that I no longer take to avoid returning to court, exposed me to an implacable litany of indictments, crucifying me on my stupid bed.

The Prosecutor-Father resembles the philosophy teacher he had at the Saint-Joseph school in Rheims, a hard man, a veteran of De Gaulle's armored vehicles, but a good teacher nonetheless, who knew his authors by heart and (despite his ice-cold feet) spoke of them *warmly*. My father claims to have good memories of that Jesuit school: the pupils played a lot of sports, the working methods were remarkable, the teachers *not terrorizing*, aside from the physics and chemistry teacher, who had a terribly *dry sense of humor* and offered him peanuts when he got a bad mark. He also had a spiritual father, a former boxer, who worked in prisons and enlisted him, for two years, in the *slum team*, refurbishing poor people's housing. Apart from that,

it was mainly a matter of making a success of and in life. It was a topic of conversation every evening. We were not to become "bourgeois" but something else, a kind of sui generis aristocracy, people "apart." That left its mark on me.

Whatever he says, the Jesuit school wasn't always a picnic. He admits, in passing, when he describes his hatred of mornings (even those when I woke him by running a brush through his hair), his love of closed shutters and darkness:

When I was an adolescent, boarding at school, waking was dreadful, at 6:00 AM, to a trumpet blast blown on a (black sheep's?) horn. It would be dark, the yard lit by high, pale lamps, and seeing us all in striped pajamas I would think of the concentration camps. All this in silence, apart from orders, before washing and morning study until breakfast at 8:00 AM. Thank you, St. Ignatius.

Of the Jesuit Father with the ice-cold feet he says that he made him *pretty Kantian*: *it was Kant and school together that sent me, rigidified, to Paris to study law.*

On his inner stage—the tottering theater where he acted out his Mysteries, sent the Evil One, Virgin, and saints out in procession, himself playing sometimes the Fool, sometimes the Crucified Man—the Jesuit took the place of the little devil with fiery hooves who teased him when he was a child and represented a joyous sexuality, untouched by fear of sin:

Around the age of 5 or 6, I would dream of the visit of a "nice little devil" who liked me and amused me, but left burnt traces on the parquet floor with his fiery hooves. On waking, I would check to see if the marks were still there, but I never saw them. At the breakfast table I would tell my dream to the family, who found it very funny, and often asked me whether these noctur- nal visits happened at the same time as naughty awakenings. The little devil has not been back since that time, giving way to desirable she-devils or trial dreams in which I was a lawyer, but always losing my robe, or wearing it the wrong way around, or forgetting my files.

Ultimately, it's carnival in the shadow theater—everything merges and spins, higgledy-piggledy, masks, roles, and cos- tumes are exchanged and combined, the lawyer loses his robe and becomes the accused, the devil wears a cassock, the black sheep takes the place of the Crucified Man, and, suddenly, a woman appears, a woman incarnating desire, vengeance, and the law, half Venus in Furs, half Donkey Skin, and, in the icy corset of fear, a little pleasure has perhaps found its niche—

To what do I owe this terrible expectation of punishment? For what has the devil in me produced a black sheep destined to

*be cut to pieces in order to make—why not—a fine coat for a
pretty lady magistrate, who thus wears her charges against me?*

K

Kabyle

Every man carries within him a promised land, a land where his feet will perhaps never take him, to which he is bound by no history, no roots, of which alone certain dreams, sometimes, bring him the colors and scents (those dreams from which we wake whole, unsullied, soothed, with the feeling of having shared a life of a higher kind, without clashes or secrets, bathed in clarity), a land to which—should he touch it one day by chance not knowing until then how to recognize or name it—he knows that he belongs, whose light and landscapes are his own, where he can move unhindered, breathe, whose stones, trees, and language charm and liberate him, as though he himself, in the mists of time, had spoken that language, been one of those trees, those stones, and the former life, the life elsewhere, seems to slip from him, leaving him naked, native, lustrous—all that time lost elsewhere, rushing, grimacing, when nothing matters but being here, living, looking, breathing, here where time no longer passes, or else passes without history or dates or years—for this is the place of a past that has no memory but from which the body is woven—in the end it's all so simple, all you need do is stay here, in this place, take root in this land, why go back?

That land, for my father, lay beyond the seas, it had the hills and valleys of Kabylia, the light of Morocco and Algeria, the bleached white of the desert. No history bound him to it, no past or genealogy, unless, perhaps (you could believe it seeing his very pale eyes in his dark face, his black hair and hooked nose), one of his Saint-Malo ancestors, long-haul sailor or corsair, had gone ashore there and developed a penchant for creating blends. But I think instead that, as a child, he must have shaped that land, without even knowing it existed, as a kind of anticountry, a radiant negative of the places he grew up in, the small towns drowned in gray and rain, the low skies, the heavy, cold air and damp earth, the heathland and stony fields of Brittany, and those old ladies in black dresses and lacy coifs who, in the cellars of his nightmares, spun spiderwebs. This land leveled by light was also, for a child who grew up during the Algerian War, the land of rebellion and danger, whose name could not be spoken at the table in his parents' house, whose violence and terrors could sometimes be described, in hushed tones, once the children were in bed—*fellaghas*, torture, faces split ear to ear in the Kabyle smile, the angel's smile—and the child lying on the other side of the wall, the child smiling like an angel in his bed, must have wondered what it all meant, hearing, too, in those adult murmurs, terror mixed with desire.

Later he went looking for that land in the cold, gray town where he lived. At night he would leave his plush apartment, his bourgeois neighborhood, to walk and walk for hours to the outskirts of Paris, to the suburbs that, for his family, his friends, had become the latest places of fear and desire, and for him—black sheep, foreigner, outlaw—the land of delirium.

I've known the search for wild pleasures and thoughtless expenditure. Around me some people bought cars in quantity, electric drills and elephant statuettes. In my case I was trying to live and relive my first Arabian tale through somnolent walks to the housing projects on the outskirts of Paris.

For hours he would walk the taut tightrope of his madness, eyes wide open to his waking dream, cars would brake to avoid him, passersby brush against him, shadows appear to ask for a cigarette or some spare change, he didn't see them, he kept on walking, straight-backed and wide-eyed, he had to go on, keep walking, to resist his inner longing to fall, and suddenly around him the too bright night of the housing projects would take on the deep black of desert skies, stars would appear beyond the beltway, the asphalt beneath his feet would be soft as sand, the concrete towers rise up like Arabian palaces.

Sometimes it was daylight, he could no longer lose himself, he had to remember that somewhere, in a quiet apartment overlooking a square, an old lady had set the table for him, that on the other side of Paris two little girls had come home from school and were waiting for him to call, or, simply, that he was tired, the tightrope he was walking (high up, so high that even the faces of the old lady and the two little girls were hard to make out) was starting to fray, and meanwhile the longing to fall was growing inside him, arms outstretched he would cling to his childhood tales, he was the son of an Eastern king, a desert prince, a man of strength and power, and, if he fell (he was going to fall), this man would catch him, take him in his arms and carry him away, back home, with him:

I have often found myself going into the salons of grand hotels in Paris to watch Arab businessmen in the hope that one of them would take me back with him, to the whiteness of the sand.

In the morgue, when I went to take him a suit and clean under-clothes, three boys were waiting by the door. Their skin was brown like his, their noses hooked. In an apparent effort to look relaxed, they were smoking cigarettes, solemn and awkward in their expensive tracksuits, heads down under their baseball caps, shoulders hunched. At the desk I heard them give the name of a housing project on the outskirts of Paris, and that of their brother, my father's twin in death. When I went back a few days later to collect the body, they'd been replaced by numerous women draped in multicolored veils. In the room where we waited, by the river, they sat across from me, filling the entire bench, shut away in themselves, singing quietly, mouths closed, rocking backward and forward. My father and the dead youth set off together, to the sound of that song, that's why I believe my father, perhaps, had his wish granted, that, guided by the dead youth, carried by that song, he could at last come in to land.

L

Léaud (Jean-Pierre)

My mother and father were at the cinema one night, sitting
side by side. The lights were already down, the film had
started, when my mother heard a seat creak behind her. She
looked back, automatically, and saw my father sit down. Yet
there he was on her right, he hadn't moved. She spent the rest
of the film (the story doesn't say what it was) wondering who
was this double who had suddenly appeared out of the darkness. When the lights came up she realized it was the actor
Jean-Pierre Léaud.

From which we can only conclude that Jean-Pierre Léaud
looks like Dustin Hoffman, or that, between the two, my father
is the link, an image left on the cutting-room floor.

I watch the character Antoine Doinel, in the different films by
Truffaut in which he appears, and there he is—the hair, the

curving eyebrows, the nose, the nervy thinness, the eternal
cigarette, it's all there—with Léaud's something extra of insolence and fragile arrogance.

I watch the entire series, on the lookout for resemblance in
this double of light and shadow.

Like the Antoine Doinel of *Stolen Kisses*, my father liked
women who were taller than he was. My mother told me that
before they got married he went out only with monumental
Swedish blondes (the woman in the photo, perhaps, of whom
only the perfectly oval face is visible), who towered over him
by at least a head.

Like Antoine Doinel in *Love on the Run*, he sometimes
also fell for petite, dark-haired women with green eyes and
sharp voices. His second wife, I suddenly realize, was the
image of the actress Marie-France Pisier. Her real name was
Évelyne Cruchot, but she called herself Ève Darsac. She was
not a lawyer (he was the lawyer), but a flighty light soprano, a
woman of easy virtue who, like Truffaut's Colette ("the girl of
musical afternoons"), would not have been above sharing the
couchette of a stranger she'd met on a train in exchange for a
few banknotes. She married my father and made him her agent
to help with her career, which was slow in starting. When they
weren't traveling to Milan they would take us, my sister and
me, to a small chateau near Paris, which belonged to Ève's
grandmother. There we would spend our time trying on her
stage costumes with her half sister, who had Down syndrome,
and refusing to call her "Mom" (between ourselves she was
"la Castafiore"). On the grounds was a gardener's shed, which
we'd adopted as our house; weekend after weekend we would
take our toys and dolls there. My father sometimes came and

joined us to play battleships with me. Meanwhile Ève would
be doing singing exercises in the music room. My sister and I
had gotten into the habit of imitating her: "pee-oo, pee-oo, pee-
oo, peeeeoooooo . . ." heads back, eyes closed, with an air of inspiration, hands following the high notes, higher and higher,
until the adults put their hands over their ears and begged us
to stop. It had become one of our favorite turns, alongside the
dance routines of *Meet Me in St. Louis* and the dubbing scene
in *Singin' in the Rain*. We would do it constantly, whenever
the silence grew a little heavy or time was dragging. One day,
in the car with Ève and my father, we started up, out of habit,
"pee-oo, pee-oo." Ève looked around, furious, as my father guf-
fawed into the steering wheel. After two or three years she left
him, taking his checkbooks with her. She also sold our toys,
our dolls, and my battleships game.

*I lived with an opera singer, who not only bankrupted, but also
anesthetized me, or infuriated me, I know not which, with her
vocal exercises from morning till night. A constant stream of
what I heard as screams would rise from the drawing room. My
spaniel would hide under my desk, as though crushed, the birds
would fall silent. I can still hear the first exercises of the morning: "hé and né and noss and nosse and nusse and nusse" etc.*

But it's in Truffaut's *Bed and Board* that I see—or search for—
him most persistently. I'm the same age as the film, give or
take a year, and so too, it seems to me, as the child whose birth
it relates. I see this film as an impossible memory, a kind of
forbidden account of what preceded my life, like the archives
of my unconscious. In it I seek clues to the story behind my

birth, which has left its mark on me, but which I can't access,
the words, moods, and qualities of light in which I was immersed, the two very young, very distant people who would
become my parents, and I sometimes seem to see them, to
recognize them, the dark-haired, nervous young man with
his tight sweaters and skimpy jackets and also the very young
woman with her doe's face, the little apartment in Paris's 15th
arrondissement, and above all the extreme youth of both, or
rather the childhood just under their skin, the impression,
sharp as a recollection, of two children playing at mommies
and daddies (Claude Jade dressed up as a housewife with her
fur hat and string shopping bag, insisting, with a little girl's
pride, on being called "Madame," and her skirts too, her blous-
es and chignons, the petty-bourgeois order of their apartment,
their docile politeness, the meals at their parents' houses, until
they tire of playing, the way children do, and eat little pots of
baby food in front of the TV, elbowing each other), that kind of
gentle boredom, the placidity of people who have entered their
lives through the wrong door, been caught in the net of adult
life before finding out who they are, I was born out of that, two
children caught out by their own game, and I feel snatches
of life with them coming back to me, the accents they put on
when they had dinner parties, the serious way my father set
about playing his role while my mother floated beside him in
a cloud of expectation and hesitation, watching, watching still
no doubt, for the moment when her real life would start, yet I
was so small I could barely talk and they were not much more
than twenty—before, just before, the apartment on the Avenue
du Maine, my father, whose talents had been noticed, was
working in a provincial prefecture as principal private secre-

tary, all day he would act Mr. Important, dealing with files or the retraining of mine workers, but in the evening he would go back to sleep in the barracks where he was doing his military service, we were left on our own, my mother and I, in the big official apartment that was dark and cold as ice, watched over by a policeman who would salute my pram. She was scared, she'd take refuge in the kitchen that was the size of a ballroom, put me on the table in my basket, call her mother and try to study for her exams by reading Barbey d'Aurevilly. Sometimes too she'd make an effort to play her part as an important man's wife, design buffets and receptions and cut recipes out of *Elle*, filing them away in big boxes of orange plastic. There was no place for youth in that life, in those days it hadn't yet been invented, they'd have their youth afterward, separately. Meanwhile two children had been born.

In May '68 my sister and I didn't yet exist, they'd just gotten married (in their wedding photos they're still so young, heartbreakingly young, touching in their grace and fragility, he wears his tailcoat elegantly but his forehead shows traces of acne and at the altar he bites his lip like a kid who can't answer the teacher's question, while she, drowned in white, her blonde hair in braids wound around her head, crowned with flowers, a bouquet of lilies in her gloved hand, she meanwhile has the evanescent beauty of an apparition, as though she's about to fade away, to return to the clouds in which her frail shapes can be seen, besides, she's not there, she's floating, but it's not happiness that carries her along, more a kind of absolute vagueness—no doubt sensed by the worried-looking mothers in their fur hats—behind the folds of her long veil her heavily made-up eyes look without seeing, a doe caught in headlights, in a state of complete stupefaction that is not, however, without gentleness, her glance slips, her eyes sometimes close, her lips open slightly in a half smile, while gloved hands write her fate in a weighty register, she dozes, lost to childhood).

Newlyweds in '68, they missed the whole thing, my mother dreamily knitted scarves full of holes for the children she was not yet expecting, he meanwhile couldn't find his role, cop or robber, master or rebel, he couldn't decide, he was twenty-two, but he was teaching at Nanterre University, he would meet docile students in a room far from the station and the girls' building, cursing the mud that splattered his English shoes, he'd seen nothing coming, really nothing at all, when the demonstrations started he went to watch, wandering around outside the university buildings at Assas, the Sorbonne, and the Panthéon, horrified by the violence of the right-wing Groupe Union Défense (*leather-clad giants carrying heavy chains, they looked like Vikings, for many had beards and long hair*) but a little too, I think, by the occupations of lecture theaters, bedlam inside the paneled walls, a speech bubble saying "Love one another" drawn on the portrait of Richelieu. In the evening he would go back to my mother in the little apartment in the 14th arrondissement and from their window they would watch the yellow glow of explosions over the Boulevard Saint-Michel. After a while she wanted to go and see. They went out into the street, but they were stopped on Avenue Denfert-Rochereau by a wall of riot police (*with their black helmets, gleaming black oilskins, long batons, and weapons, it was impossible not to be frightened*), but then one night he was the one who wanted to go, because at last he knew, he had found his role:

*My wife and I were young newlyweds and went out only once
at night. A radio announcement said that the new tear gas was
blinding students and it was vital to take gauze, cotton, and
ether to the Faculty of Medicine by any means. As children of
doctors, we were both doubly concerned. We took the car, on
which I had glued red crosses stuck to white handkerchiefs, and
we drove to the Odéon crossroads. The future doctors were clos-
ing the gates. They said to me, "Get out of here now, there's
going to be a charge." My wife was knitting in the car. I got
back into the driver's seat and said, "Watch out, it's going to be
violent." And so it was, and within a moment, because the front
rank of riot police were twenty meters away. I was sprayed by
a tear-gas grenade because I had stupidly left my window a
little open. My wife got nothing, fortunately, or she would have
messed up her row of knitting.*

Years later I too came across Jean-Pierre Léaud. He was sitting
with a glass of beer at a table outside a café in Rue Daguerre,
dazed and staring, in a kind of stupor. He was dressed all in
black and his hair—also very black still—came down in long
strands to his unbuttoned overcoat. He had aged just like my
father, gotten fatter, his face swollen by the medication that
treated the same sickness in them both.

I saw him one last time, one sleepless night, in Aki Kau-
rismäki's *I Hired a Contract Killer*. The rented video was so
worn you couldn't hear the sound, just the tape creaking. Lying in the darkness, I watched this ghost of a film, rain-swept
and nocturnal, shot through with bright colors and winking
lights. He had gotten his youthful slimness back but lost his

insolence, his humor, his arrogance. I knew nothing about him except that he was seeking and fleeing his own death.

In Truffaut's *The Green Room* Jean-Pierre Léaud does not appear, but a date is mentioned, which is the date of my father's death.

Mouton noir [black sheep]

If I had to devise a coat of arms for my father's soul (which, of course, I don't know how to do), I would represent it divided diagonally, colored purple and azure, bearing, in the upper part, a white horse and, in the lower, a black sheep. It would be "party per bend sinister, first azure a horse argent, second gules a sheep sable." This coat of arms would need to be animated to show the struggle within him of the shadow and sable, the azure and argent, the desire too to include other arms (those, for example, on the signet ring he wore when he dreamed he was the king's son). The black sheep wasn't chosen by him, others chose it for him—his family, his sisters, the white ewes, the better to banish him. Yet he made it the title of his manuscript, his impossible self-portrait, as though, among all those that inhabit its pages, the heroes and martyrs, saints and madmen, good and bad, that figure, representing his stain, his defect, or simply his solitude and strangeness, was the one with which he could best identify.

*When the description "black sheep" was inflicted on me by my
sisters, I could have smiled. I do not like stupid sheep, or the
noise they make, or Panurge's sheep that follow the herd. I am
definitely not like that. On the contrary, all around me everyone
has told me so often to "do the same as everyone else" that the
symbol of animality in me has nothing sheeplike about it. And if
it is a moral judgment on the blackness of my soul, I completely
disagree. Like everyone else I have darkness in me, but at least I
have gotten to know it, and I am armed against it. I do indeed
have a bipolar specter, and I take care of it. When it starts jump-
ing around like a figure in a fairground ghost train, I go where
I can find protection, discreetly, and of my own accord.*

The black sheep haunts his manuscript. For page after page,
it bears the weight of his raving, his madness, at night he's
awakened by its cries, its fleece adorns the woman—at once
feared and desired—whose final judgment he awaits. It's the
black sheep that, when he drinks, is *flayed alive, stripped naked by the negative lucidity of alcohol.*

And yet he tames it, domesticates it, as though, after all
these years, on the threshold of his own night, he had learned
to play with the darkness within him, given up doing *the same
as everyone else* and acting *as if,* had accepted this imposed
figure, this portrait of himself as lost sheep, scapegoat, five-
legged sheep, whatever, made room for his madness and, in so
doing, found the hope and desire that it would no longer make
him suffer, alone always, different still, but at peace:

*Perhaps one day I will be able to kick the black sheep out to
graze on the other side of the planet, so he will leave me alone in*

the world of the Little Prince to repair my engine before rising
into the sky, to stroke the fox, to watch the satellites dance.

But the black sheep restless within him is not alone. In his
inner bestiary, his freak show, there are also, alongside a fox,
some inebriated sparrows *that get drunk on the fermented*
grapes of the virgin vine and fly away chirping more loudly,
but together, sin-laden mules, frogs, and fish:

I am better in the water than on the beach, I would stay in
for hours. And I think of Paul Deschanel's burst of madness,
sauntering in tails through an ornamental pool in Versailles
and agreeing to get out on condition that he was granted a de-
cree naming him as a fish by the council presidency. A natural
request when we remember that man is descended from fish.
Perhaps the original fish sought to get closer to the sky, no lon-
ger protected by water. We know all about rains of frogs, and
Jean Rostand's interest in them.

Opposing the black sheep, there is also a white horse. This is
not a figure imposed by others, by the herd, by all those whose
number he is unable to join. When the horse appears, it's from
his dreams. But that doesn't make it a creature of terror, a nightmare ride. Where the black sheep leads him to the abyss, to the
dark side of specters and ghost trains, the white horse carries
him to the heights, into the void, into dizziness too, for, intoxi-
cated with speed and the open air, he knows he risks a fall:

Recently, in the hospital, just before my release, I had an equestrian
dream: I was galloping alone, on an Arab horse, in something like

the pampas, I had a wonderful sense of freedom, the wind whistled in my ears (riders are familiar with this benevolent intoxication). Then a very wide, deep gorge appeared, with no way around it, a magnificent river running along the bottom. The horse did not balk but crossed the great gap, as though winged, to carry me to the other side, where stood the chateau of my singer's grandmother. I rode around it to display my heroic posture, and returned through the small town nearby, where I saw bistros, vulgar women, people who seemed ugly to me, all of them.

So the white horse turns into a nightmare creature, a mount from hell, carrying him at a gallop toward all he has fled, small towns moldering in the rainy shadow of cathedrals, old women dressed in black, spinning yarn and whispering on their doorsteps, mothers with long, blood-red nails, the trampled dreams of childhood, baffled, shrunken heroes without lances or crests who have fallen in the mud, boy-kings betrayed by life, prodigal sons who return without laurels or acclaim, who have nothing to offer but the display of their decline:

In another dream I was in our old town in the provinces, near the cathedral, with my father, who was still alive, and I wanted to go farther over the rooftops into my Mother's house. There was a ladder, but I didn't climb it, because my dog turned into a magnificent white horse, which I mounted with pleasure, but noted that its left forefoot was gone and it had big, manicured fingers. Old ladies passed by and it reared up and, proudly, showed them its hand. In that position I was like an equestrian hero visiting his mother, when I was about to enter a psychiatric clinic—bizarrely located opposite my parents' former house.

It remained to him only to round up the herd of his soul, all of them—the black sheep and the white horse, the tame fox and the drunken sparrows, the exhausted mule and the flying fish—to gather them in, give them shelter, cast off their fangs, claws, fleece, give up the idea of making them into adornments, weapons, or crests, no longer pit them against each other in his personal circus, his sandy arena, just to know that they were there, buried within him with their broken legs, broken wings, to listen to their moans and their songs, to recognize his own wound in theirs, and yet, in feeling that, to feel alive.

The weakened individual who knows he will never be Goethe's hero, Nietzsche's superman, must protect his return to life by seeking out the unity of his dissociated, imperfect soul and treating the wounded animal within him.

N

Napoleon of the Far North

Back home, after disposing of his ashes, I typed his name into Google—Just another way of warding off absence, walking in his footsteps, causing an echo to sound in the void. A few entries mentioned his books, his lectures. Another talked about his death: *François-Xavier Aubry will not find himself in unknown territory. He died according to the code of the brave men of* . . . I clicked. An article opened, entitled "François-Xavier Aubry: Illustrious Stranger," by Pierre Cécil, Appartenance Mauricie, Société d'histoire régionale. It told the story of the man my father would have liked to be, the man, perhaps, that he was (you want, at such moments, to believe in past lives and lives that can start over), of whom he may have retained— who knows?—an obscure sense, a magical memory, inherited with the name one hundred and fifty years later. It was a tale of sound and fury, the story of an adventurer, an explorer, of daring exploits and high seas, uproar and glory, the kind of story you tell little boys to send them to sleep, with cowboys and Indians, faithful beasts, and fierce enemies. The first François-Xavier Aubry, the ancestral double, real and imaginary, was born, like my father, in December, to a family that, like his, was from Saint-Malo. Also like him, he was a *svelte man of medium height* (as described by Lieutenant George Breweton), fond of strong liquor, dogs, and horses. The fourth child in a family of thirteen, at the age of twelve he became an assistant at the Grand-Trompe-souris general store in Saint-Joseph de Maskinongé. In May 1843, at the age of nineteen, he left Québec for St. Louis, Missouri, and the adventure of the Far West (*a paradise for wild horses, bison, bears, prairie dogs, wild goats, and other species*, writes Pierre Cécil). Drawing on his sales experience, he became a wagon-train leader. He learned how to recruit men, pack sufficient quantities of food, water, guns, and ammunition, and select the hardiest mules and horses. He negotiated directly with New York dealers to get the best prices. Soon he grew bolder, mounting not one but two wagon trains per year: between 1846 and 1856 he organized sixteen expeditions, traveled the Santa Fe route fourteen times and the Chihuahua route twice. He moved ever greater quantities of goods—5,000 sheep to San Francisco, then, a few months later, 50,000 to Los Angeles. His reputation grew. In Kansas City and Independence the newspapers would announce his arrival to whet the buyers' appetites. The *Santa Fe Republican* gave details of his wagon trains, the *Amigo del Pais* in New Mexico published his travel notebooks. Soon his renown was equal to that of Kit Carson, Thomas Fitzpatrick, the great trappers, pioneers, discoverers of the West, destroyers of Indians, blazers of trails. Growing numbers of travelers—merchants, missionaries, gold diggers, settlers, doctors, soldiers—would congregate around his caravans, said to be the safest and fastest. He is depicted riding his palomino mare, Dolly, a magnificent beast, trained to hunt bison, sturdy, bold, and as fast as lightning, *the finest piece of horseflesh ever seen*, writes Alexander Majors, dealer in Missouri. It's said he was offered ridiculous sums for her, that one day some Indians even attacked and took her by force, and he negotiated with them for hours, covered them in gifts and money to get her back. In September 1848 he completed a mythical ride. Back in January he'd already beaten Norris Colburn's record by covering the 1,300 kilometers between Santa Fe and Independence in two weeks; then, in May, he broke his own record by making the trip in eight and a half days; this time he said he would do it in six. The newspapers were full of it, bets were laid. On September 12 he and Dolly left Santa Fe at dawn. The first of the five stages was three hundred kilometers away. He rode without a break. The Apaches living in the Santa Fe region let him pass, but the elements were against him. For twenty-four hours it rained continuously, the rivers were high, the trail was a river of mud. Nevertheless, on the evening of September 17 he arrived in Independence. He had slept only a few hours, eaten only six meals, worn out six horses. A few years later, in 1860, the Pony Express and one of its young riders, William Cody, better known as Buffalo Bill, took inspiration from his system of stages to carry the mail from the eastern United States to the West in eight days, before being dethroned, a year later, by the installation of an overland telegraph system. The historian William Vissher speaks of this ride as *the greatest physical performance accomplished by any rider of the West.* In the meantime the beautiful, blonde Dolly

had lost her life, succumbing to the arrows of Garrotero war-
riors during an expedition to California. Her master, wounded
eight times, alone and starving, had to eat her flesh to survive.
All the same, he made it to San Francisco. And it was during
that trip that he opened up the famous middle route, the Albu-
querque route along the 35th parallel. Geologists, politicians,
and Kit Carson himself acknowledged that this route was pref-
erable to the Gila route for the new railroad, which was then
at the planning stage. But the founder of the *Amigo del Pais*,
ex-major Richard Weightman, a former member of the elite
troops in the war against Mexico, known for their weapon of
choice, the Bowie knife, and for their skill in using it, launched
a campaign against Aubry. Furious at being slandered, Aubry
set off for Santa Fe. On his arrival, he went to the general store
owned by the Mercure brothers and ordered a drink. Weightman was informed of his presence and went to meet him. He
held out his hand and talks began. Tempers soon began to fray.
Weightman, a hothead who liked a duel, threw his drink in
Aubry's face. Aubry's hand went to his revolver, the shot hit the
ceiling. Weightman jumped on him, drew his Bowie knife, and
disemboweled him. It was August 18, 1854, around three in
the afternoon. Aubry was twenty-nine years old. The *New-York
Daily Times* said that he had lived two lives in half a lifetime.
"François-Xavier Aubry died according to the code of the brave
men of the West," wrote Cecil, "where every man was ready to
lose his life to save his honor. He died a hero. But he had the
misfortune to die twenty years too soon. The American collec-
tive memory has not given him the same rank as Kit Carson,
William Cody, and Davy Crockett."

It was the first Christmas after his death. We had all gathered
at a big country house with the other family, the ones who
had everything—money power fame, and the rest too, which
he had lost and so much wanted to go back to, a life without
threats, without disaster and collapse—ultimately it was just
another Christmas without him, the previous year we'd gone
to fetch him from a hospital in the Paris region, he'd obtained
permission to go out, we'd taken him for a meal, a couscous
in the nearest bistro, he'd managed, how I don't know, to find
a present for my daughter, a pink soft toy Barbapapa, the year
before that he'd come by train from Soissons to have lunch
with me, I'd opened the door and found him twenty years
older, white-haired, with a stick and a hat and his father's
clothes, we'd eaten, swapped presents, I'd been cross with him
for having brought my daughter just something he'd picked
up at home, a badly wrapped African wooden carving, I don't
know what he gave me or even if he gave me anything at all,
in the evening, like every year, we set off, we went to the big
country house by the river, log fire burning in the fireplace,
Christmas tree all lit up, seeking, in this warmth, this light, to
forget him, to console ourselves for this pain that was his nevertheless, it had been years since we'd spent the evening with
him at Christmas, performed a tap-dancing routine, a scene
from Molière or from *Meet Me in St. Louis*, even as children
we were transported on those evenings from one house to another, but in both there'd be a tree, a log fire, a family, now he
was alone, in the television room with green walls and filthy
linoleum, alone at the Christmas dinner of the mad—laughing
with their toothless mouths, blowing into their warm bubbly,
little paper triangles askew on their heads—abandoned to

the goodwill of nurses, the cracked laughter the half-baked
smiles of mental defectives and misfits, alone with those who
supported him better than we did, to whom perhaps he was
closer than he was to us, madmen in green rooms in hospitals,
tramps in tents lined up along the Seine, even in the good years
they were the people he would go to on those evenings, even if
he'd come back for a while to the other side, the side of families gathered around the warm fire of normality, on Christmas
night he would go and seek them out, share with them the now
cold turkey, raise a glass of bubbly in a parish hall, draughty
Salvation Army refectory, or charity canteen, no, no, it's fine,
he would say, anyway I saw you at lunchtime and we'll talk on
the phone tomorrow, so we would go to the other family, the
house by the river, the groaning table, mountains of presents,
trying to forget the suffering that was actually his, to console
ourselves rather than ease it, of course they told us we could
do nothing for him, we had to think of ourselves, our lives that
were still prospering in the shadow of his, I'd heard it so often,
this exhortation to indifference, to survival too, perhaps, based
on a primary truth—he's the father, you're the child—but precisely, sitting around the table with the other family before
the steaming turkey and the champagne flutes, I was still his
daughter, someone had to receive the poisoned gift of heredity, take it away from the Three Kings, emissaries of fallen
kingdoms and fallen fathers, guided, along the Seine in Paris,
through suburban hospitals, by the dark star of melancholia—in his notebook, the day before he died, he had written in
large letters *Me the impotent father*—there had to be someone
to honor that father, a part of me at least, childlike, obscure,
obstinate, to hop along with him at the party on the ship of

fools, step out of the closed circle that so calmly excluded him, honor him, share his shame and dishonor, go over with him to the side of those who, faces pressed up against the window, watch the parties to which they are not invited, the abundant banquets, the noisy, gaily colored guests with mouths wide open to snap a bit of air like fish in an aquarium, particularly as the silence, that first Christmas after his death, was deafening then, as night fell, at the time when, gathered around the hearth, warmed by the warm fire of normality, we conversed in low voices, swapped news—children, holidays, jobs, little packets of life tied up firmly with string—at the time, as day turned to night, when, before, we used to call him (what a lovely Christmas I had thanks to you, my darlings, he would say to us, I shall think of you as I fall asleep), as it got dark I broke the silence, executed a dance step, a sideways skip, to the side of the solitary the tramps the mad, to the side of the dead whose voices are overlaid, to the side of the graveless who are buried in oblivion, to the side of the fragile specters who ask for nothing, nothing but a warm breath sometimes to speak their names, nothing but a light misting on the window that protects the living, a breath, a sign that revives their absence and for a little longer saves it from nothingness, that's why that day I spoke his name out loud, François-Xavier Aubry, the Napoleon of the Far North, I said very loud as they were flicking through one of those stupid books people give each other on those days, a dictionary of names that someone had opened at the letter *A*, expressing surprise that there were so many Aubrys in Quebec, but that, I said very loud, is because of a famous explorer from Saint-Malo, François-Xavier Aubry, the Napoleon of the Far North, and the circle of silence closed like stagnant water over a stone you've just thrown into it, they thought I was mad perhaps, or trying to be clever, inventing a crazy anecdote to make them feel uncomfortable, to disturb them, but mourning isn't madness and neither is fidelity, the mad ones are those who forget and refuse to name and always act as if nothing were the matter, so I left the warm, sleepy house and the circles forming around that name that had fallen into the heavy water of silence, at the time when, before, I used to call him, I went out into the garden, already dark and rainy, down to the bank of the river rolling its yellow waters, I said sorry to him, from the bottom of my heart sorry, sorry once again for having carried his pain instead of easing it, for having suffered from it instead of loving him, sorry for having tried so hard to console myself for him.

(Ultimately, all I'm doing in writing this book is to speak his name.)

O

*I was on the right bank of a river where a house stood—and
I could see my wife on the other side, with her blue bicycle,
dressed in cheerful colors, giving me an adorable smile and a
wave good-bye. She was going toward the sun; I was setting off
from the other side, toward the rain and wind, the land of the
Dead and the priests. I went down into the cellar of the house,
and there I found some very old ladies more dead than alive,
sitting in a square and surrounded by sinister objects: skulls,
crucifixes, punctured bagpipes, models of old dismasted boats,
spinning wheels covered in cobwebs . . . This dream told me that
two worlds were parting.*

We grew up, my sister and I, on either side of a river, between
the shadow and the light, on both sides of the world—its glit-
tering surface and deepest depths, its fortunate and its griev-
ously mistreated—splayed out across two banks that moved

gradually apart, at first the gap wasn't so big and we could go easily from one to the other, every summer, at the end of July, we would leave the big, sun-blasted houses of Provence, the festivals and celebrations, to join him in Brittany, we didn't know then that he'd spent that month of July in a rest home gathering his strength for the days we'd be living together, when we arrived he had big plans, we would go sailing eat crêpes play tennis go cycling, but it was too hard, in the end, all those days of pretending, so gradually he began to disappear, in the morning he'd go down the three steps of the lounge and shut himself away in an ill-lit office, still darkened by draperies, too much furniture, and dusty books, he had work, he would say, teaching to prepare, we'd go off to the beach with my grandmother while he stayed sitting there filling in his notebooks and smoking, on our return we would tell him what we'd been doing, our cold water swims, our sand castles, we knew nothing of his day, we were pretending too—

With the arrival of the girls, whom I can still see getting off the plane hand in hand, wearing little vests with their names on them, happiness would return and a great deal of affection for a month that went by too quickly. Yet I had a terrible sense of exclusion and foreignness. My only pleasures were walking alone on the coast paths and restoring the boat my father had given me, in a boatyard by a muddy bay, buying myself a beer at 5 PM. I had absolutely no interest in that Kormoran and I don't remember taking it out more than three or four times, and with so little skill that a friend, who owned the boatyard, jokingly forbade me to go beyond the end of the jetty. I had once been a good sailor, but sickness had turned me into a public menace.

In the evenings, sometimes, my aunts would come to dinner
with their husbands and children, my grandmother would
prepare trays of seafood or roast chicken and sautéed pota-
toes, my boy cousins would tell us about their regattas, my girl
cousins their nights out dancing, it was all much more simple,
we were like a normal family, you just had to go along with it
even if, sometimes, I caught them whispering in the kitchen
about *the girls and their father*, even though I'd learned, when,
during the meal, someone mentioned the fortune of the heir-
ess at whose house we'd just spent the month of July (money
mattered in that family), to keep quiet so as not to hurt my
father, learned, also, not to listen when my uncles or cousins
bullied him, even if sometimes, when they left, I wanted them
to take me with them to their big white house on the beach,
I hadn't yet learned to live on the margins, not yet read the
books, found the words that would take me elsewhere, where
his madness would seem to me more clear-sighted than their
health, where I would be no more blinded by the splendor of
the fortunate than by the dungeons of the condemned. And
then it was time for adolescence, I was twelve, thirteen, I was
one of those girls who, on the day of the pirate regatta, waited
shivering on the beach for their cousins' friends to take them
up and away, screaming with delight, on their 420, I'd had
enough of going to bed while it was still light and the birds
were impatiently calling out in the wide, rain-washed sky, I
too wanted to go and dance with the beach girls and their pi-
rates and come back in the early morning, with bare feet and
shining eyes, to a worried mother and an angry father, but that
wasn't how it was, not at all, we were sent to bed early, my
sister and I, in our twin beds with their bedspreads of green

rep, a camp bed stood in the middle where my father would
fall asleep knocked out by medication holding our hands and
snoring, I would try to sleep while, high in the sky, seagulls
wheeled in the return of the light, I went only once to the tennis club disco, but it was with him and I was nine years old,
he was drunk and we drove off into the night, the place was
empty except for a pretty brunette dressed in black dancing
alone on the floor, when she came our way my father, glass of
whiskey on the table before him, pushed a little stool toward
her, which, with graceful movements, she avoided, smiling,
without looking at him, behind her dark hair, this game went on
and on but in the end we went home alone. He doesn't describe
this episode and we never talked about it, in his manuscript he
reinvents for me the adolescence I dreamed of:

*I shall not describe any particular memories of my big daughter
during our holidays in Brittany. She acted as mother to her
little sister, lived by day in an Olympian manner and by night
I know not how: she told me later that every evening, as soon
as my light was out, she would leave her tent at the end of
the garden to meet up with a gang of friends whom I knew
from having seen them on the beach, lying around her like the
branches of a star of which she was the center, smoking her
"cig" like a movie queen.*

This story is untrue, of course, or novelized. That summer,
I remember, I was fifteen, I wore a white dress bought at a
market in Provence and I had just started smoking, he kept a
photo of me on his desk, I was wearing that dress, holding a
cigarette, I was hanging around with young Breton boys with

soft skin and rough names, and a half-crazy redheaded girl
who said she was pregnant by a spirit, and in fact one evening
I did sleep over at her place, in a tent at the end of the garden,
we'd planned to sneak out as soon as it got dark to go dancing but there was a storm, one of those inexorable high-tide
storms, and we spent the night in our damp sleeping bags telling each other ghost stories and listening to the waves,

he doesn't say that that summer he tried to kill himself,
that the gap between the two banks grew deeper and wider,

we joined him on July 15, the previous day I'd dragged my
American pen pal out to the empty lot by Stalingrad metro station where I used to meet up with my friends to smoke spliffs
on a broken sofa surrounded by weeds and hollyhocks tall as
men, listening to rap and looking at the furious multicolored
frescoes they'd sprayed, in the evening my mother had taken
us to the house of one of her friends, the daughter of a Hol-
lywood producer, who had invited us to watch the Bastille Day
fireworks from her apartment, Lauren Bacall was there, you
could hear her rasping voice from the corridor, five of us had
dinner at a low table, the American girl and I were sitting next
to the star, she offered us a cigarette and, while rockets burst
outside, lighting up the room, she told us about life, nothing else
mattered but to find a man you could love, *Humphrey and I*, she
said, and her eyes glazed over, it was great, but even more so
because I'd spent the afternoon on the empty lot, an adolescent
vanity, but not just that, what I wanted from life, apart from
meeting my Bogart, was to move from one side, one world to
the other, without bridge or net, without belonging to either,
to be, in each, underground, a renegade, giving no guarantees,
putting out no flags, avoiding the eyes that decode and classify,

melted in, invisible, light amid light, shadow amid shadows, being myself no more than a way of seeing, a witness,

the next day my sister and I left for Brittany, I don't remember now what happened in the days before, all I know is
that one night (we were already in bed but it was still light, a
damp, misty light that smelt of kelp and hydrangea flowers),
he locked himself into the bathroom, screamed wept said he
couldn't go on, I don't know, how is it I can still see him sitting
on the edge of the bathtub holding a razor I didn't see anything
though, just heard, I ran to my grandparents' bedroom, my
grandmother, always so elegant, so polished, who only ever
left her room dressed, hair done, face made-up, leaped out of
bed, her nightdress hitched up like Baubo lifting her skirts to
make the mourning Demeter laugh, except that I didn't laugh
and it was my father who was in hell, that was something
I shouldn't have seen either, that too was the world turned
upside down,

the following days I've forgotten, we didn't go back to Paris,
the summer wasn't over, I didn't tell my friends anything, but
we left the house early in the morning, my sister and I, we
waited for low tide to walk out to the island now laid bare and
we spent hours lying on the rocks watching the waves coming
slowly in all around us.

Years later I found in books the margin where I could live, in
the ones I wrote the shoreline where I could drop anchor, in
the evening, often, I would meet up with an old writer, well,
not that old perhaps, he was the same age as my father give or
take a couple of years, had the same liking for cold seas, Brittany, and sailing boats, the same experience of drunkenness and

melancholia. He knew all about waking in the small hours in strange places, strange beds, with gaps in his memory, stretches of life engulfed by oblivion, he was familiar with the clinics around Paris and the drugs that turn the world into a wide, flat plain, no more gulfs or peaks, no collisions, thorns, or excesses, a monotonous, cushioned stupor, a life muffled, that tranquility of soul, perhaps, that the Ancients dreamed of, which makes life acceptable but at the price of boredom, that suppresses, along with the desire to die, the desire to live. Late into the night he would describe his distress, in the end I almost forgot that of my father, who must have long been sleeping knocked out by medication, we would talk about the great melancholics—angry, philanthropic, filled with pity, bold, fierce, taciturn—all fickle, Aristotle says, all highly gifted, at tables in bars we would drink the sparkling, golden alcohol that is a friend to black bile, I would give him poppies in which to bury his memories and little notebooks to preserve them, I would read him Hippocrates:

Worry: a difficult malady. The patient seems to have in his organs a thorn that pricks him, anxiety torments him, he flees the light and men, he loves the shadows, he is a prey to fear, he is harmed by contact and he has disturbed visions, frightful dreams and sometimes he sees the dead.

We would turn sickness into words, suffering into knowledge, in dark bars, over golden wines, his features would grow dim, he would disappear into himself, taciturn, overburdened, and while I recognized my familiar incapacity to console, something in me was soothed because he turned his melancholia

into art, between the pages of his books he slipped anemo-
nes and columbines and with them the magical herb, born of
Helen's tears, that dissolves sadness and resentment, brings
sweetness and forgiveness, he was supported, pampered, successful, celebrated, he strode through the world and still knew
how to find his way, in the shadow he projected he found light,
and I in that light the glory refused to my father.

P

The next summer we had left Brittany, land of the dead and priests, for the Arcachon Basin. My father was still dressed in white and went barefoot. But he was returning to the living:

I could see a miracle in myself, and particularly I was once again seeing people and things in three dimensions and in color; my eyes were no longer blinded by being turned inward, toward my past, my sorrows, my conflicts, my excesses and failures. One day I went by myself to swim in the ocean. I am a strong swimmer and passed through the spray of the high waves, then was caught in a fearsome trough that dragged me to the bottom and from which I emerged several meters from the shore, battered and stunned. I made my way back swimming crawl, propelled by fear of the breakers. Back on the beach I realized I could no longer see out of my right eye. I was given treatment and returned home with a patch on my eye, like Barbarossa.

*A few days later I took off the patch: once again I could see
everything in color and in three dimensions, which is the main
thing. It was like opening a new door to happiness on earth
after an initiation rite.*

I wondered what remained in him of the opaque, silent, somnolent world he'd sojourned in, what knowledge he'd brought
back with him. I remember little about him at that time. I was
growing up, moving away. We went on holiday one more time
together, to the South again, in Spain, then at last the moment
came when I was able to leave for good, to live far away. I
found it hard to recognize the elegant, settled, attentive man
who came over to visit me in England, called me all over the
world and took an interest in my studies and plans, who be-
haved like a father, as my own. I didn't believe in miracles.
But sometimes, in certain silences, moments of despondency,
I saw the familiar abyss. We didn't talk about it. And I felt as
though, having tried so hard to forget, my memory was now
going mad. He didn't want to remember, didn't want to know.
Or rather, knowledge fostered his great desire to forget. In
Greek the word πειρατήριον means both an ordeal and a pirate's lair. And perhaps he knew, my sorely tried father (for
the unconscious knows timeless languages and unfamiliar
alphabets), that, to return to the living, you must take off your
black eye patch and hide your initiation scars. Burdened with
knowledge too heavy to carry, he wanted only ignorance and
forgetting, indolent, colored surfaces, the infinite privilege of
ordinariness.

It was during this period that he met his blonde, laughing
Uruguayan,

a doctor and karate champion, fluent speaker of several languages, including extraordinary French, whose first name, of Persian origin, meant "she who has freed the pirate." I spent three years of happiness with my beautiful friend.

They had each had enough of traveling and unraveling. They joined forces to keep their specters at bay:

For hours we would tell each other our dreams: for her a tall ship, crewed by men from all over the world; for me, a fine three-master, like a Newfoundland vessel, sailed by women (touché!). Sometimes on going to bed she would have profound attacks of despair thinking about human suffering and the unbelievable gulf between her country's great wealth and the poverty of the people, her sick, separated parents, and the childhood dream that often recurred, in which Charlie Chaplin fell to his death from a window. To take her mind off it, I would get some socks, put my hands into them, and, hiding behind the bedpost, make them into puppets. She would play too and, as I had two telephone lines, she would call me from the bedroom, put on a sepulchral voice, and say, "This is the voice of your past life" etc. It was neither good nor bad, it was all just nice, and amusing.

They rented an apartment, bought a dog, built dikes against villainous, undrinkable waves and *piratical ideas*:

You have to accept your fragility. Sadly piratical ideas from the past sometimes turn up unexpectedly.

After three years, the ideas came back, all the more violent for having been contained, and drove them apart. He was dragged even further down, knocked out, doubly blinded. But once back on the shore he wanted, this time, to deposit his knowledge somewhere. In the newfound land he had reached, the little white room in which we'd gathered the relics of his past, he composed his writing, in two parts: "Ordeal" and "Hope," day after day he wrote these pages that, in my turn, I'm trying to decode, whose language I try to hear and understand, looking for signposts in my familiar alphabet, resonances in this past he has novelized, order and meaning in our shared chaos, drawing on his words, his phrases, his memory, until I'm no longer able to tell whether what I'm pirating in this way is wisdom or madness.

Q

Qualities (man without)

At the end of his life my father didn't want to be anything. By that I mean he wanted just to be, to take off his masks, cast off his rags, abandon the roles, the characters that throughout his life he had expended so much effort in playing, shed the qualities he had put on one by one, seeking the one that would define him, give him form and content, that would at last turn him into his own statue, a silhouette of marble with clean contours, sharp lines, a person, a complete man, a man of quality, one of those who stride through the streets in the broad light of day without ever wondering why they are themselves and not the shadow that clings to their footsteps, and so he went on, writing new titles on his visiting cards, trying on his clown's red nose, his spy's glasses, his pirate's eye patch, his black sheepskin, his Freemason's apron, eternal five-year-old boy juggling possibilities, standing in front of the mirror striking the poses of imagined lives, searching for the life that would, at last, stick to his skin, imprint itself on his features, the life in which his inner crowd could come together, say in a single voice *this is me*, but, however hard he looked, he never found, there were too many of them, the others he housed, too many of them living inside his skin, speaking with his voice, it was they who, each in turn, through him, said *I*, qualities without a man, attributes without a self, atoms dispersed around an absent center.

And so a day came when he wanted to be rid of them, even if it meant going naked, even if it meant being nothing, a man without qualities and even a little less than that, or much more, just a man who, in spite of everything, lived. For this he had to give up having things, which wasn't easy in a family where a life was valued in houses and furniture, in property and acquisitions. In the small white room we'd moved him into, he had nothing left but a couch and desk, a few photos, a few pictures; and of all the many branches of his family, he could count only his children as kin:

I have not yet returned to the world of pleasures, but I know that joys are possible as long as you go toward them. Rediscovering closeness with my family is already a "great joy" and I cannot hope to <u>have</u> that of enjoying Montaigne's library, Dalí's swimming pool in Cadaqués, Napoleon's little field desk to write alone looking out at the sea, the breakers of the Pointe du Raz, the bursting waves at Biarritz. To <u>be</u> once more the beloved, esteemed father, to find love by <u>being</u> once again seized by it. Having: I don't need much. Being: I must be able to <u>be</u> again, fully, but differently no doubt. All I can do is make this promise to myself.

You might, on reading these lines, understand them as an edifying story, a plan for saintliness. One of his friends, whom he saw shortly before his death (for in the end he had met up with an old friend, his last), described things to me this way. But my father was not a saint. And what was at stake in those last months was not redemption, salvation, or forgiveness. What he wanted was to rediscover joy, what he called *great joy*. Just being, in other words, having life flow through him once again. I don't know what that meant to him. For there's nothing more private and at once more anonymous than that particular power, which transports you at life's beginning, when endless possibilities glitter, and which we rediscover, perhaps, only at the end, when it has been exhausted. I don't know what form it took for him, whether once again, like an adolescent, he carried within him a vague, violent expectation of love, or whether, as at the birth of a child, he'd once more been seized by an overwhelming, trusting love, or indeed whether he no longer needed all that—being a father again, a lover again—to be dazzled anew, to feel, when he got up in the morning to write, or went out to buy food at the market, a plenitude, a lightness that were foreign to his memory, his past, as to the small details of his day, a gratuitous, impersonal, groundless joy, of the kind that carries you to the crest of the world, filling you with the tireless desire to take the measure of it (by walking, writing, whatever), the great, burning desire combined with satiety that is perhaps pure apprehension of life.

I also think, though I may be wrong, that, at least in those moments, he had given up not just being someone, but being himself. That he was ready to shed not just masks, attributes, qualities, but even the one who bore them (or at least to stop looking for him, the self who had escaped him all his life). He was already naked, bleached, purified, and dried, like a piece of wood battered by the waves for too long and at too great a depth. Now he was exposing himself to the void. Suddenly the void he had feared all his life—improvising barriers, erecting simulacra, scribbling in notebooks—had filled him up, and he was fine with it, he was at peace, as though nearing, at last, his promised land, his white desert:

Why too, in these circumstances, have I found a little peace? Away from the guerrillas of the past, unknown to all, without a label. It could go on like this for years.

Here again I don't know what, in all of this, is wisdom, what is madness. When he wasn't well he no longer knew who he was; and now he wanted to be no one, he was returning to something like health, full health, won from the abyss, from stifling exhaustion, the health you can achieve only by passing through such things, fighting the angel, spending time with your demons, encountering, if only once and at the risk of your life, something greater than yourself. And it is perhaps in this full health that the uncertain line between wisdom and madness is blurred, that there's no longer any sense in distinguishing between the one who shatters and scatters, peopled by too great and too noisy a crowd, and the one who, by dint of control, eventually reaches his own summit, no longer needs to know who he is. And so it occurs to me that, though my father may not have been a genius any more than he was a saint or a sage, he did have his share of a rare and precious experience, that, having never been fully part of himself, having known the pain and joy of that particular rapture, he came very close to what is described in a few black, luminous books, and obscurely in his own too; even when everything had left him, and thanks to that dispossession itself, in them he always had brothers, always had fellows.

Revenant

Shortly before my father's death I met up with a man I'd once been madly in love with. Back then I was eighteen, he was much older. He had courted me by sending me armfuls of roses and a book on Theseus with the subtitle: "The Power of Specters." We met that evening at a party held on a boat by people I vaguely knew. It had been snowing all day. The night was quiet and resonant and the city through which we glided, anchor weighed, seemed frozen, hollow and artificial, like a set cut out in steel. I went up on deck to smoke a cigarette. A man was standing there, leaning on the rail, hat pulled down to his ears. He started talking to me, eighteen years on, with the same feverish volubility, and his voice echoed in the snowy silence and the emptiness of all those years of absence. We went down to dance. He took off his hat, his hair, once flame-red, had turned gray. A few weeks later he asked me out for lunch. We met in a restaurant near the

Champs-Élysées. We did what you do in such circumstances,
we tried to describe those years to each other, eighteen years,
nothing really, but twice the age I was when we were lovers.
Afterward I walked for a long time, in the still fragile light of
the coming spring, in a state of shock and amazement. There
was cruel trickery, a betrayal, the mark of a mocking god,
in the sweeping aside of those years, the insinuation of that
past into my present, the appearance of this man in the snow
telling me he'd never stopped loving me, as though for my
part, in order to grow up, I'd never had to turn him into a
memory, to outlive the girl he had possessed and who, because she was nothing, back then, but her passion for him,
had been obliterated with that passion, as though, to grow
up, I'd never had to abandon the pair of them, the girl and
her lover, fused without reserve, clear out the places they'd
lived in, the world they'd created for themselves, erase one by
one its celebratory signs, the magnetic centers to which, back
then, they'd been drawn, the Saint-Jacques Tower, the Theseus in the Tuileries, the ancient queens of the Luxembourg
Gardens, the Square des Arts-et-métiers, long ago drawn into
their lovers' conspiracy, as though I'd never had to reduce
them to insignificance, a simple backdrop for the life that
continued and that, in spite of everything, had belied what
they'd said—he that never again would she love like this,
she that she couldn't live without him—as though I'd never
had to sort through letters and notebooks to turn them into a
book the way you erect a headstone, learning to distinguish
between what, in the two of them, I wanted to preserve and
what had to be buried, finding a link between mourning and
inheritance, fidelity and forgetting.

The day after that lunch I learned of my father's death. It had almost certainly occurred (the police and doctors told us) the day before, had come upon him in his sleep, or just as he woke up. So I couldn't help thinking that my father had died just as I was going to meet this man who'd returned from my past. Having been such a firm believer in meaningful chance, so keen on signs, I no longer knew, in the daze of mourning and this concurrence, whether in fact it was a sign, and how to decipher it, a punishment, a consolation, a sleight of hand, or the sovereign irony of mocking gods. Over the weeks and months that followed, on several occasions, by chance, in the street, I met friends I'd long lost touch with, classmates from my school days, and it was as though, through these meetings, something was restored to me, the right, perhaps (whereas separated from my father, I was cut off from my childhood, living in a flat, hollow present, without foundations), to something like roots, depth of field, continuity with the people I'd been, proof, ultimately, that the past never passes.

And I saw my old flame again too. We hadn't changed as much as all that, a bit more cautious perhaps, more restrained and civilized. At first it filled us with joyous incredulity and then, gradually, a bleak sense of scandal. That body, that face, so little changed despite the gray hair, had been deserted by my desire, they no longer contained the whole world, so he was no longer the same, and no doubt nor was I, we were made of different components, other loves and other people, we seemed the same but we'd been entirely reconstructed, like Theseus's ship, even though, through us, two memories were trying to meet, two ghosts to come back to life.

So through this man, who was present and very much alive, this man I'd found again as I was losing my father, I was mourning something else again, experiencing the disappearance within the living themselves of the lost people we carry inside us and who are ourselves, engulfed by time, erased by the continuation of our lives.

S

SDF [no fixed abode]

He went off barefoot, my grandfather told me that day on the phone. It was my thirtieth birthday, I was surprised he hadn't called. That evening I was having a party in the country, in the big house by the river. There I was, in the kitchen, making quiches and cakes, the baby was asleep in her wicker basket on the table, I told the friend who was celebrating her birthday with me, my father has disappeared, he went off barefoot, and again a few days later, back in Paris, to explain why I was late to a reading, my father has disappeared, the words I uttered dropped into silence, perhaps I should have said them differently, in a confiding or lamenting tone, not like a breach opened onto what I had always hidden from everyone, those words had no connection with the language I spoke, the language others understood, any more than they did with that kitchen where a baby was sleeping in the scent of melted chocolate, or with the Paris theater where, however, an actress was reading words that were mine too, that

I had written a few months before, those words seemed to have been heard by the woman sitting beside me who had just turned her head away, tight-lipped, but I didn't understand anything, I had just one phrase in my head he went off barefoot, perhaps it was from that one phrase that all the others stemmed, perhaps I'd only ever written to make it audible without having to say it, but the connection was missing, the operation of translation between that phrase and the others, that phrase and the rest, that phrase and me, and those to whom I'd said it (but perhaps in such a way that they didn't understand it, without giving it tone and intention like the actress at her lectern who was saying my words in her voice), those people weren't helping me find him, turning away, embarrassed, tight-lipped, as if, before their very eyes, I had taken a bandage off a wound that wasn't properly healed, in that silence my father disappeared a second time, and I went with him, I know not where, I followed the phrase, or not even that, just the word *barefoot*, it was all I could see, dirty bare feet below frayed flannel trousers and all around, a mess of images, the stock character of the vagabond, bag hanging from a stick over his shoulder, the obscure, royal Wandering Jew, the deserted banks of the Seine at night and also, above all, human forms lying on the sidewalk, wrapped in cardboard and plastic bags.

(As a child in the late 1970s I'd seen a report on a man who had decided to stop wearing shoes. He said that to protect his feet he covered them in some kind of blue paste. For months, in the street, on the sidewalks, I would look for blue footprints.)

Now I know (and of course it makes me feel better) where my father's footsteps had taken him. I follow them, reading his words:

Running away, running away from a masters class, taking
a train without a ticket, walking in the stream of cars from
Saint-Germain-des-Prés to the Arc de Triomphe, diving at night
into a polluted river, walking, walking, and keeping on walk-
ing through the night without identity papers or money to the
ghettos just outside the city, and finding myself at daybreak in
an African shelter, then kindly returned by taxi drivers to "my
Father's house" with a big smile and a good night, my darkness
lit up by very white teeth. (There is no Society for the Prevention
of Cruelty to Animals for dog-men who are lost without a collar
. . . It's a prison cell or the Police Psychiatric Hospital.)

He had within him an ancient fondness for the lower depths.
My mother, who said so little about him, told me that one day,
as a brilliant young man full of hope, he had told her he would
end up on the streets (and I remember too that when I was
eighteen, a proud, wild kid who stalked the streets head high, I
was often hailed by the homeless—"Little sister!" one of them
called out one day, "I know you, you're my blood sister!").

One evening as I was passing the Folies Bergère, well dressed
and at a commanding stride, on my way to meet my operatic
girlfriend, a homeless man in his sixties called out to me, "I
used to be like you, pal!" It was said without malice, more as a
friendly warning, a piece of good advice.

So, walking through the streets head high, he too met homeless prophets (it was—by my calculations, matching up our
chronologies—around the same time) like this one, suddenly
appearing outside the Folies Bergère, this one who kept him

from his madness or perhaps looked after it, for it was his
madness that bound together conquest and loss within him,
dreams of glory and the desire to fall, it was his madness that
carried him to the top of the world to hurl him down all the
harder, and off he went, boy-king, beggar-prince, off he went
barefoot without a trace, crossed the cold, opulent streets
of Saint-Germain-des-Prés, smiled, perhaps, in a stupor of
stories and the dark glory of dispossession, at his reflection
coming and going in the windows of the clothes shops, this
mature man, dressed in tweed and flannel and walking barefoot, walking, walking in the stream of cars, deaf to the honk-
ing of horns squealing of brakes screaming of insults, perhaps
smiling still, for there was victory in that walk, after all it was
leading him to the Arc de Triomphe, a long intoxication, more
tenacious than that of bad wine, an irresistible freedom, in the
end it's so easy to be rid of everything, you only have to take
off your shoes and everything becomes a lie, the provocative
luxury of Saint-Germain-des-Prés, unobtrusive, respectable
fathers, the calculated steps and pedestrian crossings of bourgeois journeys, it takes almost nothing, a bit missing in the
uniform, a clown's nose on a lawyer's desk, to cut a slit in the
world, to show that you aren't part of it.

Barefoot, my father went over to the other side, the side of
those who are instantly noticed by people who instantly look
away, the human forms lying on the sidewalk and also those in
whom we have no interest after the late nights and early mornings when they clean offices and erect buildings, the workers
from that elsewhere we'd like to send them back to the way you
get rid of a worn-out tool, those who were spoken of, around the
table in his family, with that hostile fear that adopts an expres-

sion of scorn, those whose simple mention could lift a prohibi-
tion, so that at the end of the meal racist and lewd jokes would
mingle in the same mood of transgression, it was those whom,
leaving his *Father's house*, he was going to join. It was to them
that his bare feet were taking him, beyond the bounds and lights
of the city, in shelters into which, their work over, those of black
and mixed blood pour, far from the white body they irrigate, far
from the streets and apartment blocks they've built, out of sight,
it was to them that he went, those with no money, no papers,
homeless, and that subtraction that is used to name them (as
though, like the God of negative theology, they were excluded
from the world to such an extent they could only be referred to
by denial), this privation-made-name defined his new belonging. He who, at the end of his life, wanted to have nothing so
he could just be, from whom I received the works of Meister
Eckhart, I like to think (but perhaps I'm just trying to make myself feel better) that in that shedding, that dispossession, he had
already found what he would later call the *great joy* or at least
(and of this I'm certain) an ecstasy, an exit from self. In those
shelters far from his *Father's house*, he invented perhaps different forebears for himself, a family without legacies or roots,
which adopted him for a night before taking him back home,
lulled and somnolent, like a child asleep in the back of a car
in his parents' arms. It was his dream of the desert that he was
pursuing, barefoot, in suburban shelters and Parisian bars, his
combined desire to break away and to be adopted, which was,
perhaps, none other than a way of dying to himself in order to
give himself new life.

It so happens (I'm matching up our chronologies again)
that I too visited those shelters, at around the same time, and

demonstrated with those who lived there, visible at last, in broad daylight, in the city's main streets, that was the subject of the piece that the actress was reading. I talked to him about it too, but of course he didn't tell me anything (and I'd have been pretty shocked if I'd met him one night in a shelter, sitting on a camp bed with a plate of *mafé* stew). I'd lost track of him, but I was still trailing him. Again there was a silent transmission from him to me, a complicity. And if I felt so at home on the margins it was also perhaps because I saw him there, because I knew it was my lineage.

A few months later, he went back to live in the provinces, dividing his time between a large apartment with a garden and the psychiatric clinic opposite his parents' former house. We went to visit him, my sister and I. The three of us walked through the deserted streets of a Sunday afternoon, as we had done as children with our grandmothers, through these streets formerly affluent and calm, where, after mass, they'd take us to buy good things for Sunday lunch (we'd be pressed against their furs, our eyes devouring cakes—*religieuses* or *saint-honorés*—and marrons glacés, savory *pâtés en croûte* and *terrines de sanglier*, while they discussed the weather with stylishly casual salesgirls), streets now sad and gray, lined with dirty shop windows and run-down cafés, blighted, like the entire town, by unemployment and decline. My father was wearing a green Barbour jacket, hat, and gloves, he walked slowly, a little absent, leaning on our arms, a noble old man. We walked past a group of men sitting on the sidewalk with a German Shepherd surrounded by plastic bags and beer cans. One of them, older, bearded, a cigarette butt stuck between his lips, raised his can to my father and, considering us, my sister and me, briefly and ironically, asked him hi there, all right? as you would a friend in the street, yes thanks my father replied without looking at him, gripping our arms and increasing his pace, it was obvious that they knew each other, and what was also obvious was that my father hadn't leaned down toward him, one Sunday after mass, holding out a small coin in his gloved hand the way Barbour-jacketed gentlemen do, but that the day before, perhaps, he'd been sitting there with them on the sidewalk, or on a bench in a square somewhere, sharing beers and cigarette butts.

In that town where I had gone to seek refuge or my grave, I know not which, it was a very sick man that people saw and identified, while I wandered through the streets wearing an Indiana Jones–style hat, leaning on a stick I had painted white, because I was afraid, of skateboards, of cars, of all those tall Picardy people who talked loudly and filled up the sidewalk on market days, afraid of falling. In short, half madman, half tramp, particularly on Sundays in those periods when the bank frowned on me and I would go and pick up cigarette butts outside schools. I was so hungry one Sunday lunchtime that I went to the hospital to beg a sandwich and was given a bar of chocolate as well.

What he wrote there, what I understood that Sunday afternoon I already suspected, of course, because with him I'd always feared the worst and that's one of the forms it takes. My life, at that time, was partly haunted by what I suspected of his but didn't want to check. Transcribing these words, matching up our chronologies, I rediscover both his memories and my own, and that silent contagion that bound me to him, immersed in his misery, carried in my father's misery like a baby in its mother's belly, but being crafty like him, moving closer to the bull's horn the better to slip out of reach, absorbing all the air, life, and light that still filtered through, and reading his words I suddenly understood that, born of him though I was, that misery was his.

But how can I accept that he was sometimes hungry, walking to the hospital from which, when he was a child, his father would return to preside over the bountiful table at which unfolded the weighty ritual of Sunday lunches, how can I understand the energy and attention to detail he put into his decline? When we went to visit him, my sister and I, alerted by too long a silence or that way he had, on the phone, of telling us not to worry, he would receive us in his big, tastefully furnished apartment opening onto a garden where squirrels played, or in the comfortable clinic where he had a small room papered in pale pink and decorated with engravings, a three-star hotel, he used to say, whose calm, comfort, and cuisine he would praise. What did I hear, one day, in his silence or his way of telling me, on the phone, that everything was fine, that made me insist so strongly that he must come and have lunch with us in Paris one Bastille Day?

There were times when I felt at ease only in a quiet café in the center of town (the one where, long ago, I used to buy my mother's cigarettes). That was where I used to go to try to settle the big question of "why have I sunk so low?" with, when I could afford it, Belgian beer, which, for a while, made me forget my

anxiety, before my return to the white coats or the big apart-
ment with its silent telephone and empty letterbox (when it was
full I would throw the mail away, as I no longer wanted to exist
for anyone, feeling my death approaching). But I wanted to
kiss my children before going to the graveyard of the elephants
or black sheep. It was for that reason that I accepted my elder
daughter's invitation to go and see them for the fourteenth of
July in Paris.

The man to whom I opened the door that day had aged fifteen years. He carried a stick, with a hat on his now gray
hair, his body thin inside a baggy, crumpled suit. He was very
late and smelled of alcohol, he confessed that he'd stopped
at a bar along the way. He could hardly stand, didn't speak,
didn't eat. I got him to lie down on my bed, windows open
to the bright light of summer, I tucked him in and I called
the emergency psychiatric unit. The doctor stayed with him
a long time. You've got to get him to the emergency room, he
told me, he's dehydrated and suffering from malnutrition, he's
very weak, and he gave me a prescription on which I saw the
letters BD. I didn't understand what they meant at first. It was
the first time that letters, not even a word, had been applied
to what he was suffering from. So that was how, that Bastille
Day, we found ourselves in the emergency room of the Pitié-
Salpêtrière Hospital, a stone's throw from the apartment where
he'd long ago lived with his singer, on Boulevard de l'Hôpital,
and which he'd chosen, perhaps, because, in the provinces,
his parents lived on Rue de l'Hôpital, Pitié-Salpêtrière, the
name of which, when I was a child, called up an image of
leprous walls, crumbling, pitiful walls. We were told to sit in

a corridor painted dirty beige and chlorophyll green, there
weren't many other people there to start with, a few children,
some pregnant women, and then, toward evening, through the
sliding doors came, along with the distant noise of celebra-
tion and fireworks, the pungent breath of the summer night,
staggering brawlers with slashed, smashed-up faces, homeless men, their feet wrapped in rags tied up with string, in
one alcove nurses kept dumping stretchers, from which hung
the naked, blotchy arms of old men hooked up to drips, those
who had brought them immediately disappearing as though
all that could be done was to dump us there, everyone out this
is the end of the line, standing, sitting, lying in this corridor in
the neon light absorbed by the sickly walls looking at the big
clock with its hands that kept on turning even though time
had stopped passing we were there for all eternity, a young
woman, dark-haired, pretty, wearing a white coat, was walking smartly toward the exit, I stopped her by the sliding doors,
is it true about the BD? she asked laughing as the doors closed
behind her, a stretcher was free I lay down next to an old lady
with terminal cancer her bones visible under her green shirt
her crumpled paper skin dappled with big brown blotches, my
sister had turned into a nurse she was turning with the hands
of the clock, faster and faster, rushing to see if anything was
needed, pulling up blankets, bringing glasses of water, sitting
beside me my father wouldn't eat or drink or sleep or move, he
had his eyes open, fixed on the space in front of him, he was
calm, heavy, like a fallen stone, a tall man came through the
doors in handcuffs flanked by two policemen his clothes torn
his cheek swollen and an arrogant air they took him into a
corner out of sight, shouts metallic rustling a falling body, the

old lady listened in silence her eyes wide open, mind your own business they said to me, we're doing our job he's dangerous we've given him a going-over he's a wife-beating asshole mind your own business, at four in the morning the door I was lying by opened, my father went in and me after him, everything's fine the doctors said he's just had too much to drink he's just tired go home to bed anyway we haven't got any more beds, I don't know what I said to persuade them to keep him in, perhaps that I didn't want him to throw himself out of the window or lock himself into my bathroom to open his veins, perhaps that I wouldn't be able to stop him, nor how, the next morning, with the help of a doctor friend who'd known him as a child, I found a clinic in the Paris region that was willing to take him and which he left, a year later, calm, reconstructed, and alive.

In the metro, when I see homeless men with rucksacks, clean and clean-shaven, I wonder what superhuman efforts they must have made to wash, change their clothes, clean their shoes, where they spent the night always afraid someone would steal their things, what time they got up to be able to go to a public bathhouse, what hot food they have eaten. They often look lost, eyes turned inward. What do they see? A wife, children, parents, bad luck ultimately. Writing this I am ashamed of my breakdown in the town where I grew up when I wanted to throw away all the opportunities life had given me, and the ones I had preserved. In a way, my attitude was indecent. A psychiatrist in a clinic said as much to me one day, looking at my filthy English shoes with trailing laces, "You're a tramp, you're putting your misery on show." Another had said, during my previous time out, thirty years before, "You are a professor, so act like a

*Professor; you are also a lawyer, so act like a Lawyer." I was
Boudu the tramp saved from drowning, when I could at least
have looked like the Epsom Gentleman who had trouble paying
for his hotel room but who set off for a day at the races dressed
like a prince and used small scissors to cut the fraying threads
from his shirt. Obviously those men had not abandoned their
own selves, they had found their place in the world.*

T

Traitor

To the already veiled promise in the eyes of the little girl with
blonde hair cut anyhow whose photo he kept among his papers

to the two syllables that I hear my daughters babble and
that I have not said for so long, to all they imply of trust,
strength, tenderness, and presence

to the memory that returns, sharp and clear, one sleepless night, of his smell, his warmth, his arms around me when
we had to part, those moments when he was, yes, a rampart,
strength—when, like anyone else, I had a father

to the daytime world when his arms should have carried
me, to solid ground, to life in the light, untouched by hell

to the magical signs he would trace on my forehead, to the
amulets, exorcisms, protective charms, drivers-out of black
sheep and demons

to sweet lies and blessed blindness, smooth surfaces, to
quietness of mind and benevolent selfishness

to what his shape itself, or the name by which we called
him, should have promised, a world unbounded, ignorant of
that other world into which his shadow cast us

(daughters, sisters, and accomplices of those who walk
barefoot on the dark side of life)

to still seas, scenes without mystery, faces without masks

to voices that say "I" without trembling, to changeless,
gleaming portraits in their worked frames, with mocking
smiles, proud of their resemblance to themselves

to linear narratives, to familiar alphabets

to lives framed by two dates and which unfold from one to
the other without rebirths or disappearances

to burials, to engraved headstones in the quiet of cemeteries

to the lightness of the earth

to the stone that anchors memory and to the mourning it
contains

to the forgetting that filters the mingled waters of memory
and from which they spring, purified of obsessions.

Traitor

as I am too in writing this

transcribing his words (*To be novelized*)

to silence, to secrets, to appearances that must be kept up

("In his case," wrote Marie-Ange Malausséna, sister of Antonin Artaud, "there is no reason to speak of vice. Nor, more-
over, of heroic experience. We must simply say nothing." And
Dr. Latrémolière, the Rodez intern who was writing a thesis
on electroshock therapy while administering it to him, twelve
hundred in three years, said, "I didn't make literature with
Artaud, you understand, I made life. I had a live experiment

with him.")

to all that I don't say

to all that our mingled lives have deposited in me, silently

fractures, shards, rubble

tenderness, desires, and choices

(adding, in the margins, my crosses and crossings out to
his, surrounding the lines through which he recomposed himself with codes and protocols of my own devising, cutting his
portrait into a puzzle, piece by piece, the complete picture still
unknown to me)

to his enigma, his opacity

to all of him that is unknown to me, and always will be

to all my dead, to all the dead, loved and unknown, those in
whose warmth I grew up and those I will never meet

since to all I must, as to him, swear fidelity.

U

Utopian

As a jurist, my father was a specialist in decentralization—which, if we take the state as the self, was not without its consistency. He had, at a very young age, written a brilliant thesis on the subject, founded an academic discipline, published books and articles. At the end of the foreword to his first *Essay on Decentralization,* he writes that, in his analysis of the *weight of the "centripetal state,"* he was unable to silence his personal beliefs, since it is impossible *for writers to hide their Egos behind their pens.* In the last pages of his manuscript it is this man, the jurist, who takes up the pen. With the same meticulousness he once put into his teaching and his law books, he outlines a new society, point by point, a society of the excluded, the vulnerable and ill-adapted; he imagines a city in which they would have a place, city halls that would be *everyone's home* and where elected representatives would receive the mad; he draws up a list of volunteer groups, emergency services, telephone help lines, even if, he says, the most important thing is *a warm place to get one's Unity back, in other words solidarity with oneself,* even if

the main structure is first of all the "Ego" and in its shadow the Jungian dragon holding in its jaws the keys to the city, in other words, the place where men live and work together.

He praises at once the welfare state and libertarian movements, he, former man of the law, confirmed Gaullist who, in May '68, had been so afraid of chaos, sees those *events* as *signs of a mutation in the Spirit of the Times* and a *divine smile on the modern soul.* He doesn't go so far as to dream of revolution—everything within him has already been so far overturned, he wants to see the seed of this new world in the world he is starting to reinhabit. He cites the foreword to the European Constitution, and notes that it mentions *the weakest, the most deprived, minorities,* and their *protection* (he's looking for a constitution for those who don't fit in a particular box, who no longer have one):

These elements are the precursors of a change in societies, which one hopes will be easier to bear for those who have suffered, to the point of falling ill, from the imperfections of the system as it is known and submitted to, or of their ill-suitedness to it. These texts drawn up for citizens of whom the majority, if not the totality, are regarded a priori as normal, signals an advance in political philosophy with the introduction of the notion of common good and, lastly, and less modestly, of a "principle of good."

He has read Hannah Arendt, seeing in her work *the true philosophy, the philosophy of reference.* In *The Human Condition,* he finds both diagnosis and remedy. What else has he faced, in his melancholia, but the temptation of contemplation and, in his rejection of life, what Arendt calls the *vita contemplativa*? What else has he done, in losing the world, becoming foreign, alien, to it, but seek refuge in himself like those who, in days gone by, were called sages and who, he wants to believe, shared his madness?

The man who wanted to avoid the sufferings of the world went, among the Ancients, "to alienate himself" [sic] in relation to himself: a flight from the business of the world and crucially a refuge in the inner citadel where the self is exposed only to itself. This is no different from what I have experienced, diving into myself and taking refuge in psychosis. It was, with hindsight, a kind of mad abjuration of life on earth.

V

Void (master of the)

I fled, endlessly walking through the night. Back home all I could do was sleep, then return to myself by sheer force of soul, as they say, the impassive soul in the dress of Mr. A, wearing a ribbon, accepting my sickness and the end written into it. I dressed and sat down at my work table, I was Mr. A reigning in his Empire office like the master of the void of a buried city.

W, (or the memory of Childhood)

The phone rings one evening, late, I have just found out I'm pregnant with my second daughter. A man's voice, gentle, almost tender, calls me by the name they used for me when I was a child. I can find no image corresponding to this voice, nor to the name of this man, which I have read, however, since my father's death, in a letter of condolence. You've forgotten, he says, but I remember, we lived right above you, you used to come up and see us, you had a knack of turning up when I was in the shower, we adored you, you used to sparkle, we used to see a lot of each other, as a foursome with your parents (so my mother and father were still a twosome then), we used to have lunch together, dinner, we used to go on holiday together to the house on Île d'Oléron, your father loved that place, it was heaven on earth, we live in your apartment you know, when you left (when they left each other), we moved in, we've kept the green paint in the hall, do you remember? And that little

room at the end of the corridor (yes, I remember, it was my
father's study, I can still see him shut away there writing his
thesis, one day when I was tired of seeing him working I threw
his glasses out of the window), that little room is my bedroom
now, you can come over you know, whenever you like. The
gentle, faceless voice goes on speaking, lulls the baby I'm carrying that I've just been told about, it houses her in an older,
mellower past, but also, hearing it, suddenly the world doesn't
seem to be pitching and rolling so much, there's an anchor
touching the bottom, as though I too were rediscovering a land
and a past, from that age that had vanished with my father, for
no one else ever talked to me about it, the age in which my life
is rooted but which, for my mother, has been covered over by
another life, so there is still a witness, a person for whom they
were two, and I was with them, *shadow among shadows, body
near their bodies*, this faceless voice gives me a memory (for
I don't have memories of childhood, the angry little girl who
threw the glasses out of the window, the one who would wake
her father every morning by running a brush through his hair,
the girl who, one day, on the doorstep, gave him her favorite
toy, pretending she didn't understand that he wasn't coming
back, I know that little girl from a distance, I don't recognize
her and couldn't call her by my own name, she's more foreign
to me than the one I'm carrying even though I feel an uneasy,
distant affection for her, mingled with remorse as for a child
whose eye I'd caught without speaking to her, but now it's too
late and she's no more than a shadow, a vague outline with
no content, there's too much space between me and her, too
much of the shards and rubble), this gentle voice calling me
by my name gives me a present, it's as though, listening to it, I

can start inhabiting my own life, I who, I suddenly realize, am
in my life as in a foreign land, having arrived without luggage,
why here and not somewhere else I don't know, perhaps that's
why others and elsewheres are familiar to me, the broken ties
to my memory my past have found somewhere more distant
to hook up to, an immemorial, impersonal past, that childhood
language, learned from their voices together and that I can no
longer speak, has been replaced by others, ancient languages,
the languages they call dead, whose alphabet has reached beyond my own to anchor me in a shared past, anonymous and
personal, a shared birth, and now I've been given back a land
that's very close to me, for the voice speaking to me echoes
around the walls inside which I grew up, to this voice they're
not backdrop and rubble, but the substance of life itself, like
the city where I was a child but where I always feel I have just
arrived, this city too is suddenly familiar to me, more solid,
more complete, of course I know that neighborhood, the avenue where we lived, and the apartment block I've walked past,
with the door it never occurred to me to open, any more than
the doors you see in Italy, painted in trompe l'oeil, in those
paintings that hide the facades of ruined churches, two years
have passed since that phone call, I haven't seen the man who
spoke to me that evening, haven't responded to his invitation,
but what point would there be since his voice in itself was
enough to take me home.

X

Xavier

My father bore a double given name, sonorous and complicated, one of those names that unambiguously signify membership of the bourgeoisie. My grandmother was always very
careful to say it in full. Two years before his birth, in the winter
of 1944, she'd given birth to a stillborn baby, named Hervé.
And while she hadn't given her second son the dead baby's
name, or called him *Rene,** she had chosen a double name,
as though also baptizing the dead boy, treasuring two sons in
one body. For the sake of ease, many of my father's friends
and family called him by his second given name, Xavier, and
sometimes he too (for example when he was telling jokes,
adopting, for the occasion, a Spanish accent) would refer to
himself that way. No one called him François and it would

---

*"Reborn" in French.—Trans.

never have occurred to me to recognize him in that name. One day, on the phone, when he had already been living in Soissons for several months, he announced to us, my sister and me, that he intended—in his apartment that was too big, too empty since the death of his father—to put up a young man by the name of Jean-Maxime, very nice, a reflexologist by trade, with whom he would share the rent and meditation sessions. We'd heard other fantasies like this, another week and it would all be forgotten, but we did wonder what this one might mean—a significant meeting, friendship, dream of adoption, even love, who knew?—the hypothesis was disturbing, but reassuring all the same, at least he was no longer alone, someone would be watching over him. Days passed, weeks, and Jean-Maxime was still coming up in our conversations, he occupied my grandfather's room, doing shopping and cooking, inviting friends around, organizing parties, life was starting up again, my father said, I feel I've found both a son and a friend. Soon Jean-Maxime himself started answering the phone, do you want to speak to François? he asked me that evening, I hesitated for a moment before realizing that it was my father he was calling by that name.

The day my father collapsed in the street, brought down by a heart attack, it wasn't Jean-Maxime who told us, but the police. We tried to reach him to find out what had happened, but the phone just rang and rang. The next day though he did come and join us at the hospital, with clothes and washing items. He was small, he looked like a kid, dressed entirely in denim, with a shaved head and bright, evasive eyes. He spoke in a very soft voice, which didn't fit with the rest—any more than his English shoes fit with his faded jeans—he had a casual air, a distance that, at first, I took for reserve. He came with us to the station and suggested we go for a coffee while waiting for the train. The guys propping up the bar seemed to know him, he greeted them, chose a table by the pinball machine and ordered fruit juices. He sat very straight, turned slightly to one side, and in his soft voice he began talking to us about our father as though he were someone we'd known slightly and lost touch with, François is a good guy he's going through a bad time he needs to learn to relax he's too anxious don't worry we'll get him out of there he needs company the rent I pay him isn't expensive I can put some money aside for a consulting room no no let me I'll get it OK if you insist, see you.

We set off reassured, we needed reassurance so badly. When everything kept on getting worse, up until that Bastille Day when a ghost rang my doorbell, he told us nothing. He didn't tell us that my father was drinking himself to death, collapsing in the street, no longer had enough to eat. We went back to Soissons one last time to clear the apartment. Jean-Maxime had already moved out. He had cleaned the windows and the bath. We left him books, crockery, clothes that wouldn't fit in the boxes and the Bulgarian ambassador's Mercedes so he could look after it until we sold it (a few months later it went for scrap). Going through papers I found a set of photos: a man who must be my father, clearly drunk, with a blurred, lost look in his eyes and a can of beer in his hand, Jean-Maxime next to him, each with a girl on his lap. On the back a name, François, and a date, December 31. I don't know who took those photos, nor do I know who that François was.

Y

The letters are running out, this meaningless order in which I've tried to hold his disorder and mine, to smooth out our memories, to spell out, tentatively, the very ancient knowledge that I haven't found, as though these words, these sentences, written under the impulsion and necessity of a different order—his—an injunction or promise (*To be novelized*), would, once finished, fall apart, return to their primary elements, scattered, disconnected letters, a constellation of letters exploding across the sky of oblivion, of impossible coinciding, impossible fidelity, and I too, in pieces, inarticulate, return to the speechless age before the ABC of memory, so many other narratives are possible, other orders, other codes in which to encrypt what I still can't decode, this writing he left still has the urgency of voices that have fallen silent, and it seems to me that I could keep going through it forever, could endlessly recompose it, what would happen if I closed it, what will hap-

pen when I close it to put it away, finished business, with his
diaries and notebooks, this writing in which his voice still
sounds and through which shines, weakly, the black sun of his
melancholia, this writing he would so much have liked to pub-
lish and which is now once more a *dead letter*, what emptiness
then, and how many books must be written how many stories
novelized to fill or return to the void that opened three years
ago to the day, today (and this morning, on the anniversary of
his death, I received my birth certificate, needed for another
mourning, another dossier to file away, the certificate drawn
up the day after my birth "on the declaration of the father" and
signed by a state official named DESIRE), this void into which
I instantly knew I would throw words, his, then mine, then
both together, mingled, a fragile bridge, very high, suspended
over absence and leading me back to absence, a bridge woven
of our bifurcating memories, though they were born in that
ancient, stumbling age when our voices were assembled like
the two prongs of a *Y* springing out of the same stem, the *Y*,* a
dead language in its name, *Y*, symbol of the unknown, of that
which, in him as in me, will remain forever foreign to me,
that which no book, no alphabet recomposed with throws of
a dice can name, the letter that the Greeks used to refer to the
symbolon, the two fragments of a ring broken in a friendship
pact and that, in their precise fit, signified recognition.

---

*In French, *Y* is called *Y grec*, meaning "Greek *Γ*."—Trans.

Z

Zelig

He's the little man you see in the crowd, running away, always running away, and who wears the crowd's colors, brown shirt that day among the brown shirts, a Nazi among the Nazis, he was also black in a jazz band, Native American inside the bars of a reservation, green with orange hair in an Irish pub, a rabbi with the rabbis, Greek coming out of a taverna, I saw the film when I was a child, I remembered the human chameleon, I'd forgotten that Zelig is mad (on a platform, to the crowd that first jeered and now cheers him, Woody Allen shouts: "It shows exactly what you can do if you're a total psychotic!"), I'd forgotten the scenes in the psychiatric hospital, the straitjackets and white coats, the psychiatrist played by Mia Farrow, and the meaning of that madness, being like the others to be loved by them, I remembered only the escapes and transformations, the motley in black and white, the man who endlessly eludes himself, as though madness were not the key to him, any more, perhaps, than it is to my father, nor to the portrait, the impossible portrait, that he tried every day of his life to create, that I have taken on in my turn to defer his death, this portrait from twenty-six angles with an absent center, this portrait in twenty-six others with a self that eludes it, my father wasn't like other people, he was other people, he didn't want to be loved by them, he was looking for the man in himself that he could love, they all inhabited him at once (he would tell a joke: How do you kill a chameleon? By putting it on a piece of tartan), the Black Sheep and the Napoleon of the Far North, the Jesuit Father and James Bond, the Cop and the Traitor, the Madman and the Sage, all forced to cohabit in one body that through them died a thousand deaths and lived as many lives, all together in a single presence now gone, I have called up this troupe of masks once more with my sheep's horn, but it still lacks the presence that brought them together, the body they inhabited, the voice, the laugh, the eyes that brought them to life, all those things that I can't call up or spell out, whose traces can't be carried by words but only, set and cold, the photos that I still can't look at, he refused a grave, a stone, the mask of effigy, and the final face, he preferred ashes scattered to the four winds, perhaps he has found, in the white desert of death, that which he always sought—the right, at last, to be no one.

Belle-Île, March 26, 2009

GWENAËLLE AUBRY's previous novels include *Le diable détacheur* (1999), *L'Isolée* (2002), *L'Isolement* (2003), and *Notre vie s'use en transfigurations* (2007), which was written while in residency at the Villa Medicis in Rome. In 2009, she won the Prix Femina for *No One*.

TRISTA SELOUS lives in London, where she works as a translator and teacher of French. She has published many translations and is the author of a book on the novels of Marguerite Duras.